THE LONGEST NIGHT

BY

JOSEPH A. WAILES

OUTLAW PRESS
RAWHIDE, TEXAS

OUTLAW PRESS
2980 PHYLLIS LANE
RAWHIDE, TEXAS
75234-6425

THE WINNER OF THE HUMAN RACE

BY
JOSEPH A. WAILES

I_WHEN LIGHT BECAME A MAN

II_THE LONGEST NIGHT

III_ANCIENT DREAMS, NEWBORN VISIONS

IV_WAR OF THE BOOK

V_THE THIRD UNIVERSAL EVENT HORIZON

VI_HARVEST MOON

VII_TOO GOOD TO BE UNTRUE

BOOKS AVAILABLE AT OUTLAW PRESS

TABLE OF CONTENTS

DEDICATION

This work is dedicated to the Name, the Word, and the Power of the Living God. Father, Son, and Holy Spirit could be another way to describe this Person, Who made us, saved us, and will glorify us. For now, we glorify Him.

FOREWORD

When a farmer steps out onto his porch at sunrise, his eyes scan his land, as far as he can see. He knows what he will likely see, and is looking for something out of place, in case he needs to do something about it.

When he finishes lunch, and thanks his wife, since he thanked the good Lord before he ate it, he steps out onto his same front porch on his way back out to work. As his eyes scan his land this time, it is still the same land, but appears vastly different in the noonday Sun, than it did at Sunrise.

When his workday is done, after he has finished his supper, again with the appropriate thanksgiving, he steps out onto his porch again, and moves over to sit down in his chair. As he leans back to relax, and let all of his sore, tired aches ease off a bit, and review what he did and did not achieve this day, his eyes scan over the land again. This time it looks even more different than at noonday, but it is still the same field, and still the same Sun, and still the same man looking at it. The only difference, other than time, and the farmer's fatigue level, is the angle of illumination. If the farmer were to walk across the field all the way, and look back toward the house, it would look radically different than all the other views, though still the same field, Sun, man, and so forth.

The hope of this work is that the reader will perhaps be able to see, or consider, or at least consider the possibility that there still might be much undiscovered, and un-mined buried treasure hidden inside the Word of God. Bring along your Bible, and an open mind, if you want to see, too.

THE GREATER LIGHT TO RULE THE DAY

It had been building for a very long time. This was, after all the third generation. The first had been a super-giant, with a relatively short life span of only two and a half billion years. Then it became supernova, and for a few minutes, was the brightest light in the visible universe, expending the majority of its' total energy all at once.

The dust and fragments spread, cooled, condensed into solid matter, then larger and larger clumps of solid matter, then huge masses of solid and gaseous matter, until finally the entire mass was large enough that gravity began to pack the pieces tighter and tighter into a giant, dark, slowly spinning disk. Slowly is a relative term, here.

Eventually, a new star lit the night sky, this one also a bona-fide super-giant, but not nearly as massive as the original star. This one had a longer and calmer life span, and lasted almost four billion years, before the fuel supply of hydrogen in the star began to be harder to find, and the internal pressure, from the constant detonation of thousands of hydrogen bombs every second, became less able to support the general structure of the star against the crushing pull of gravity. Finally the entire star caved in upon itself, and the combination of compression from the collapse, plus a time-delay restraint against the release of the internal pressure, as the intense gravity field held the explosion longer, and longer, making it grow bigger, as still more fuel was gravity-injected into the furnace, continued and accelerated, until an insanely high level of internal pressure in the collapsing star reached a sudden snapping point, and in the blink of an eye, LIGHT happened all over the whole universe, and the debris and dust spread, and the whole process began again, on a smaller scale.

As the grandson star was forming from the leftovers of the second super-giant, all of the heavy elements that are only produced in supernovae were swept up into the mix, as well as hydrogen and helium, and everything else of normal matter. As the core sections of both the newly forming star and each of the planets condensed first, the heaviest elements were gathered in the centers. The dense centers had strong enough gravity pull to also collect all other sorts of solid and gaseous material. The dense centers soon became completely covered in layers of atmosphere. This deep atmosphere was present upon each planet, all the way to the still dark star, which was itself covered with a thick atmosphere. The entire solar system, if seen edge on, would resemble a flying saucer with a very large bulge above and below all the rest, largest at the very center. The planets were all gas giants, even Mercury, Venus, Earth, and Mars.

The planets would also be visible as lumps in the disk, but are all so small compared to the sun that they would not be noticeable to the naked eye.

The whole thing was a dusty, smoky dark mess, until the baby star one night had enough material, and enough pressure from gravity, and enough raw fuel as hydrogen to sustain a continual chain reaction detonation event.

IGNITION!!! The new star exploded, but with only a fraction of its' total power. This star did not become supernova, but actually sub-nova, even though nova does mean new. Even so, the light-up blast was the most spectacular explosion ever seen, so far, in the entire history of our solar system. The outward force in all directions from the sun was more than just blindingly bright. If there had been ears to hear it, it would have been the loudest bang so far ever heard in the solar system, as well.

This event was not just about the flash-bang show. Real devastating force was also released, and made sudden and permanent changes in the entire system. Mercury had started out as the very largest planet, making Jupiter look tiny by comparison. Venus was only a little smaller than Mercury. Earth and Mars were huge monsters, too.

The outward blast tore into each planet. The ones closest to the blast lost the most. Similar in a way to the trick where the waiter snatches the tablecloth out from under the items on the table, and they remain in place upon the table, the same sort of visual could have been observed as the shockwave tore away almost all of Mercury's mass, shredding and blowing away all but two percent of the original Mercury. The same effects occurred in the case of Venus, Earth, and Mars. Venus was left with four percent,

Earth with seven, and Mars with eleven. The heavy cores of the planets were rocky and dense, and their own heavy mass gave them enough inertia that they remained in orbit, just vastly smaller, and lighter.

Some of the material from the planets ended up forming the asteroids, out at a distance that was about where the light-up blast had diminished enough over distance (inverse square law) that the gravity pull from the sun could hold them into orbits. Some of the particles made it out to Saturn, and helped to form its' rings. Some of the chunks made it out to freeze and become independent comets, with individual orbits of their own.

Most of the asteroids and planetary rings and comets are oriented, and remain, in the general flat plane of the solar system. The debris which was ejected from the sun itself went out in all directions, however, and traveled far out beyond the planets, and formed what we now refer to as the Oort Cloud, though no one has yet been out that far to take a sample of the material. If they ever finally manage to do so, the odds are that it will prove to be star-stuff.

Although science cannot verify nor disprove every single theory that exists, some of them do not need to be proven. I do not know the secret name that Jesus said when He called our sun to life. I do know that it is His voice which will raise the dead some day. Since we already know that He will do that, how much easier was it for Him to say something like, "Sun, LIGHT!"

TWO EVENINGS EVERY DAY

The majority of the folks in the world do not spend a large portion of their lives upon the ocean, though many millions do indeed live along the coastlines. Sailors know things about the oceans and the sky that they learn from older sailors, and also from experience of their own. Some of those sailors also study oceanography, and learn the currents and the extraordinary and strange ways of the ocean waters. Others study the marine life more than the actual structure of the ocean, or its' complex fluid dynamics.

Most folks are not aware, for example, that a strong, tightly concentrated current flow runs along the equator down on the floor of the sea. The forces involved with that phenomenon are directly linked to the rotation of the earth, but are still not the strangest current known to exist.

Hidden within this undersea river (which is larger, and much swifter, than the Mississippi), runs another smaller, faster current, a second undersea river, moving in the precisely opposite direction from the larger outer shell current. No one has yet been able to accurately measure if there are still more layers of current hidden deeper within the layers.

Another scientific fact about the ocean is the pattern of the tides. Most folks probably do not realize that there are two even tides per day. There is even tide number one, followed by high tide, followed by even tide number two, followed by low tide. The entire cycle repeats every day, and a graph of the pattern would be a regular long sine wave.

The two even tides occur as the change occurs between day time and night time. High tide happens at sunrise, low tide happens at sunset. There is the first eventide, followed by morning, and there is the second eventide, followed by night.

The day begins at sunrise. That is why in the ancient world, 9:00 A.M. was called the third hour. That is also confirmed in the gospels where it is recorded that the women came to the tomb "early in the morning, on the first day of the week, as the Sabbath was ending."

This is also made evident in Genesis, if the literal text is read precisely enough to perceive the connection. It is recorded, "And it was evening, and it was morning, day one." This can only logically be understood as the first eventide, followed by sunrise, and the beginning of the day.

If this were not the correct understanding of the text, would it not then more accurately have to read something like "and it was evening, and it was sundown, night one"?

I suspect that a whole lot of the misunderstanding develops from the fact that most people are not up, and at sea, or even down at the beach, in the early wee hours of the morning, and therefore do not ever realize that there is a dual eventide, every single day. It must be one of those things that will be right there in front of us all the time, hidden in plain sight, just to teach us to look a little bit deeper.

That is also made obvious by the timeframe that the Lord Jesus took up His life again. His resurrection was the brand new beginning of a brand new world, and He chose to accomplish that miracle very early in the morning, before sunrise. On that particular day a Son brighter than our closest star, the Sun, arose from a dark death to shine the renewed Light of His second life into our lives. As there had once been a Day One of Creation, that day was Day One of Salvation. When He returns to judge the quick and the dead, it will be Day One of Glorification.

NOBLE FAMILY LINES

When the Lord decided to bring all the animals before Adam, he was instructed to name each of them, just as the Lord had named each of the stars of Heaven. Adam was still uncorrupted by sin, and saw things as he was designed and built to do. When the wolf came up to him, Adam saw the future of the wolf, as well as his present, and knew everything there was to know about wolves, just as with each of the other creatures.

Adam looked at the wolf, and smiled, and said," You are Wolf, and will be the most loyal of all the creatures in the earth with Man, even to the point of your life for his, lovingly given, if needed. Man and Wolf will love each other forever."

Sometime later, as the animals continued to come before Adam (with Wolf curled up beside him) an unusual little horse-like creature appeared in his turn. The moment Adam saw the Donkey, he said, "I see who you are, little Donkey! You are the Bearer of Truth, and will carry the King of Kings into War in times to come! You shall one Day become the Warhorse of God!"

Sometime later after that, things went very wrong in the Garden, and also for the whole world. Nevertheless, the prophecies of Adam still held true. Over the millennia that followed, Wolf and all his descendants, in all their artificially-modified forms, from nervous little dogs that would fit in a hand, to enormous, clumsy things, almost the size of a small horse, continued to love and help men, in ways no one would have guessed, and only God and the prophet Adam had been able to see. Donkey and all of his descendants also helped men, again, in ways only God and Adam had known before.

Many times throughout the centuries, the sons of donkey had carried heavy workloads, and many people, including Abraham, and most of the Holy prophets of God. Wolves had helped in individual families and persons, once domesticated and acclimated to humanity. Donkeys were, however, the ones directly involved in the pivotal, major moments in the history of mankind.

Even before the King of Kings was born, He was carried, while still within His mother, Mary, upon the back of one of Donkey's sons. The donkey safely and faithfully bore the unborn King to Bethlehem, and, right after He was born, also carried Him all the way to Egypt, in His mother's arms. This was to escape the murderous madness of a pervert known as Herod. Years later, the same faithful donkey carried Him all the way back to Israel, this time to a new town, to start a new, hidden life, away from the nosy, evil hearts of the current rulers of Jerusalem.

The old donkey stayed all his life with the same Holy family, and had some sons and daughters, also. Joseph gave one of the daughters of the donkey to a cousin of his in Bethsphage, a town at the Mount of Olives. That she-donkey was a wonderful, gentle friend to everyone she met, and delighted people always, being especially fond of, and gentle to, all the children of the village, and spent most of her happy days constantly giving them all rides all over the village area. Joseph's cousin was very happy to have her as a great babysitter with the little ones, since she was smart enough to never wander off, or let one of them fall, and was ferociously protective, and had even killed a wild pig that had come too near one of the little boys once. They did not make her do any hard labor, since they had other, bigger donkeys that did not mind doing it, when handled gently and respectfully. When she was all grown up, they allowed her to fulfill her dream of having her own little one, and chose the large boy donkey that she had shown a strong liking toward. A short time later, they had a fine, strong boy colt. He showed both his daddy's mighty strength, and his mother's extraordinarily gentle disposition. He was not a wimp, however, and even before he had reached a year old, had earned the respect of each of his fellow boy donkeys in the town, and none of them would dare try to shove him away from the feed trough.

One day, when he was about two and a half years of age, and mostly full grown, two strange, quiet men came to the house a little after sunrise, and began to silently untie him from the hitching post. He did not feel any fear or unease, though. It seemed like he had been expecting them for a while, and was glad to see them. His mother, also tied next to him, was more concerned, but somehow seemed to suddenly know that these men would cause no harm at all to her baby. She also calmed down at once.

Joseph's cousin, now older, and slower, came outside to see what the noise was about. He asked the men why they were loosing the colt, and they stopped, looked calmly at him, right in the eye, and said, "The Lord has need of him."

That statement froze him in his tracks, and then he also slowly smiled, and said, "Then we give him to Him, with our blessings!"

He asked the men if they would stay for breakfast, but they politely declined, stating that the King was waiting for them, and advising that the man and his family should rise and quickly head for Jerusalem, to choose a good viewing place along the main street to the Temple, since the King would be arriving there shortly. Joseph's cousin gasped with excitement when he heard this, and thanking the men, turned and hurried inside to waken all the children and his wife, to get them up, dressed, and fed, so they could get going.

A few hours later, they were thrilled to see the spectacle as Jesus stormed the stronghold of evil, and rode into battle on their own little gray donkey. Along with all the other Hebrews there, from all over the world, in town this week for the Passover, they, too shouted "Hosanna! Blessed is He who comes in the Name of the Lord!"

Thousands of years later, upon the Great and Notable Day of the Lord, King Jesus leaped onto the mighty back of His resurrected-into-glory little gray donkey, now transformed into the most fearsome and powerful mount of any horse that ever lived, with mighty, great wings of his own, and flames snorting out from his nostrils as he breathed, and great streams of fire from his mouth whenever he roared his war cry. His eyes had become like his Masters', white-hot lasers that bored into whatever he stared against. His fur glowed white hot also, and he shined in glory, slightly less than the King's.

As the King aligned His Army to prepare to charge, at His right hand rode Adam, mounted upon the resurrected-into-glory donkey that had carried Mary and the unborn King into Bethlehem one special night. At Adam's right hand also came Wolf, also resurrected into great glory, and shining, too. Wolf had become a terrifying spectacle to behold, and was a creature that even a T-Rex would run from, screaming, to escape.

At the left hand of the King rode Eve, mounted upon the resurrected-into-glory donkey that had been the sweet and protective mother of the little gray donkey. At the left hand of Eve also came She-Wolf, the mate of Wolf.

As every resurrected Saint of Heaven and every resurrected creature of the earth came to silent attention alongside the King, all the Holy angels of God, and the three Holy cherubs of God, joined the Army of Heaven, and formed into alignment, also.

The King of Kings raised His unbreakable Sword of Truth, a Blade burning with His Own Glory and Power, for it seemed to grow right out of His upraised Arm. As He did this, every single voice of the people, angels, and all the entire Army shouted in unison with Him," Blessed is He Who comes in the Name of the Lord! Holy, Holy, Holy!" As the last word was shouted, shaking apart the earth, and cracking open the dark sky to pure Light, the entire Army of Heaven followed the King to the earth, to finally kill the wicked, forever!

PRECEDENTS OF THE ARK

The project was nearly complete. For over a century, Noah and his family had been building the great ship, the very first ship ever in the whole world. It did not much resemble what the navies of the world would later build and sail, since the purposes of the world are always different than the purposes of God, and this ship was God's ship.

Form follows function, as a design principle, and so the Ark was much like a very long, thin rectangular box, almost a gigantic square tube of wood, and it was entirely closed up, once Noah raised the hatch and sealed it closed. It was the size of a modern aircraft carrier. It was essentially a giant wooden skyscraper laid down on its' flattest side. Even flat on its' side it still towered the height of a five story building, one that was seventy five feet wide, and as long as one and a half football fields. These precise proportions are tested and proven to be the most seaworthy and stable design guidelines for a sea going vessel, and made the Ark virtually impossible to capsize or sink. Nothing less than a super tidal wave would even have any chance to destroy the ship. This design also greatly reduced roll and pitch, even in very rough waters, so that the occupants of the ship were not continually thrown from side to side.

At the time Noah was commanded by God to build the Ark, most of the creatures with flesh bodies that dwelt in the earth, including almost all of the humans, had acquired a taste for violence. People killed people, animals killed animals, people killed animals, and animals killed people, all mostly for sport, and a twisted desire to inflict horrible pain and death upon helpless victims. God looked down from His Throne, and one day decided He had seen enough. Extermination was demanded to fulfill justice, and only Noah and his own family, and the decent animals that did not constantly rejoice to do harm to each other, were to be spared. The rains began on what would later be celebrated as the Passover, and continued for forty unimaginable days and nights, non-stop, a continual world-wide thunderstorm.

The spies sent by Moses into the Promised Land were there forty days and nights. Jesus was in the wilderness forty days and forty nights. The Hebrews wandered in the wilderness forty summers and forty winters. Forty years after the Resurrection of Jesus, all of the gospels had been written by the eyewitnesses, and the prophecy Jesus said about the devastation of Jerusalem, and the destruction of the Temple, had just occurred.

The Ark was at sea for months, and came to a stop when it gently ran aground on the top of Mount Ararat. The precise day that the Ark touched land was later celebrated as the Yom Kippur, the Day of Atonement. The day that the waters had receded and left behind some dry land, and some mud, was later celebrated as the Feast of the Dedication. The day when Noah had his first drink of new wine from his new garden was later celebrated as the Festival of the First Fruits.

The dove which Noah sent out to look for dry land is a fore sign of the day when Jesus was baptized, and John, His second cousin, saw the Holy Spirit of God descend like a dove from Heaven, and land upon, and remain within Jesus.

The dove returned with a leaf from an olive tree the final time she returned to Noah, and then she returned to him no more after that. Jesus was standing upon the Mount of Olives, in the Garden of Gethsemane, which means olive press, when He was arrested, and willingly, by His Own death, as full payment for all the sin of the whole world, brought about the return of mankind to God, for the final time, since sin could never again separate God and man after the price was paid in full the next day.

The things God did in Genesis with Noah and the Ark set the pattern and timetables for even the Hebrew High Sabbaths and Feasts. They even indicate much about what would happen throughout the history of Israel, and in particular the life, death, and resurrection of Jesus Christ.

EXTERMINATION

Abraham was sitting under the shade of the trees in the cool of the late afternoon. He had pitched his tent near the summit of the small mountain of Alon Mamre. This oddly beautiful little mountain was situated only about five miles away from the "cities of the plain," which were named Sodom, collectively, as the smaller group of towns just a few more miles to the north were called Gomorrah. Abraham would have nothing at all to do with any of them, since he pitied them as perverted abominations, crammed full of thousands of psychotic, violent criminals. Down on the plain, those folks really had escaped from the crazy-bin, and locked up, or tortured to death, all of the sane people who dared to speak out against the constant, brazen, done-in-broad-daylight evil. The only surviving sane person in either group of towns was Lot, Abraham's nephew, along with his family. It may be thought by some that Lot was pretty much out of his mind, also, to make his family live anywhere near such perverts.

As Abraham looked westward, noticing the very unusual cloud formations, he thought it would be one of those few in a lifetime spectacular sunsets that are some of the best blessings in life. Suddenly, walking seemingly right out of the glare of the bright afternoon sun over the other mountains to the west came three mysterious men. They all wore the same plain gray robes, with their hoods drawn, even though the day was not very cold. Abraham was instantly fascinated, and drawn irresistibly toward the Man in the center, a very tall and strong Man, and there was something extremely familiar about His stride and movement. For a split second, the breeze blew the hood up a little to reveal the eyes of the Man, and

Abraham gasped. Those eyes were pure white light that did not blind or hurt, but seemed to draw one deeper in, as though into an endless pure white tunnel of light.

As soon as the feeling returned to Abraham's hands and feet, and his heart stopped thundering in his own ears, and his breathing started up again, he calmed his shaking, as quickly as he could, and eagerly ran to meet the Man. He could not stand still; he had to do something, at least. When he reached the Man, he fell on his face before Him, and said that if it would please the strangers, it would be his honor to offer them refreshments along their journey. The Man accepted with a silent nod, and a quiet smile.

Abraham escorted them all back over to the terebrinth trees around his tent, and asked Sarah to prepare things for their guests. They all sat down outside, and waited, while watching the pretty sunset begin to glow, as it turned more and more beautiful, but with a strong percentage of deep red mixed in it.

Sarah finished the meal preparations, and brought out everything to them, and gave it to them all, then returned to the tent to make the desert ready, while the men talked about their strange matters. The Man warned Abraham not to go anywhere near the cities of the plain, but to move out in the opposite direction. He then told Abraham that a year from this day, Sarah would conceive and bear him a son. Sarah was old, but she still had excellent hearing, and heard what the Man said, even inside the door of the tent. She only just barely managed to stifle a laugh, and if she had been drinking a glass of milk, it would have sputtered all over the place. The Man instantly looked at her, but, instead of seeming angry, He smiled. He looked back at Abraham, and asked why Sarah had laughed. He explained that He would do whatever He said He would do, and at the precise time He said that He would do it. Sarah had returned with the desert, and protested, claiming that she did not laugh, but the Man smiled at her again, and said, "No, but you laughed!"

After desert, He led Abraham over to the view overlooking the cities of the plain, and told him what was about to occur. The two other men with the King began to walk down the mountain side of Alon Mamre toward the cities. The one that had been on the right hand of the King was the mighty cherub, Michael. He was there to forcibly whip the devil's butt, if it tried to interfere with the scheduled execution. The other man, which had been on the left hand of the King, was the General of the angels, Tzedek-el. This was the designated executioner, and it was a long career for him, stretching all the way from the Garden of Eden, until the very last evil creature was eventually thrown into the lake of fire to die, at Judgment Day.

Sometimes, the fulfillment of justice required the shedding of blood, and the ending of evil lives, and Tzedek-el was specifically designed for the nasty job. He always hated killing anything, but also would not tolerate evil to live and to hurt good creatures.

The General only killed when and what the King told him to kill. Tonight was to be a total sterilization of a sick filth that was infecting that entire region of the world with foolish evil. He had been commanded not to use actual nuclear force against the doomed cities, since in the centuries to come, many children of Abraham would live and travel all over that area, which (after the climate change caused about 536 A.D. by the super-volcano, Lake Toba, in Sumatra) would become known as the Dead Sea, and be turned into a desert landscape, as would almost all of the Middle East, as well as Northern Africa.

As the two heavenly executioners continued toward the target, and the bloody sunset deepened into dark blue twilight, Abraham continued to speak with the Man Whom he had met before, and Whom he realized was the Lord God Almighty, standing with himself as just another Man. Abraham pleaded with the Lord to spare the people in the cities if God could just find 50 righteous men there. God agreed. Abraham then asked the same if only 40 righteous could be found. Again, God agreed. Abraham then asked the same if only 30 were found. Again, God agreed. Finally, Abraham asked if God would spare the cities, if only ten righteous people could be found. God once more agreed, but told Abraham not to push it any further, but to get packing, and get moving, even RIGHT NOW, away from the cities, and not turn back, or look back there again, not until morning. This time, Abraham agreed, and started to turn to go pack. Although it is not recorded in Genesis, perhaps Abraham, like Moses in later times, at last asked the Lord, "What shall I call You? What is Your Name?"

The King of Kings must have smiled again, and said, "Melchizedek."

The translation of that Holy Name is "Savior-Almighty God-Creator-King of Justice".

PROMISES BEARING GIFTS

Genesis 12

[1]Now the LORD had said unto Abram, Get thee out of thy country, and from thy kindred, and from thy father's house, unto a land that I will show thee: [2]And I will make of thee a great nation, and I will bless thee, and make thy name great; and thou shalt be a blessing: [3]And I will bless them that bless thee, and curse him that curseth thee: and in thee shall all families of the earth be blessed.

Romans 12

[6]Having then gifts differing according to the grace that is given to us, whether prophecy, *let us prophesy* according to the proportion of faith; [7]Or ministry, *let us wait* on *our* ministering: or he that teacheth, on teaching; [8]Or he that exhorteth, on exhortation: he that giveth, *let him do it* with simplicity; he that ruleth, with diligence; he that showeth mercy, with cheerfulness.

When the Lord first called Abram, He gave him many promises, after first ordering him to get out from his country, which was Ur, and from his father's house, and away from all of his relatives. Abram did leave, but also took several of his family members along for the ride, which later proved to be a troublesome and costly choice, as some of them eventually brought a ton of problems into existence, that would otherwise likely not have ever occurred.

The first promise was that God would make of Abram a great nation, and as a sign of that, before too long, God changed Abram's name to Abraham, meaning "Father of Many Nations."

The first listed gift of the Spirit is prophecy. God certainly fulfilled that first one, and indeed, the descendants of Abraham are a significant portion of the total population of the earth today.

The second listed promise is that God will bless Abraham, and He most certainly did do that. The second listed gift of the Spirit is ministry, or literally, healing. The healing arrived around two thousand years ago when the Son of God came to town. While He walked among people, He performed more cures and healings than anyone had ever seen or heard before Him, and of more powerful and profound kinds, of any and all types and degrees of severity of disorders, sicknesses, injuries, and demonic infestations.

The next listed promise is that God will make Abraham's name great. Indeed, the good Lord has also fulfilled that pledge. God has even caused one of the Children of Abraham to be given the Name that is above all names, whereby we must be saved (YSWH.) The next listed gift of the Spirit is teaching, and with the arrival of Jesus and the Gospel about Him, the whole world was taught the Way of Salvation. Certainly, that must be the greatest knowledge ever taught.

The fourth listed promise is that God would cause Abraham to become a blessing. We have abundant evidence to prove the fulfillment of that promise. In fact, most of the world's present civilizations are patterned upon either Old Testament Laws or New Testament Commandments, or a combination of both. People could have never built stable nations and cultures without correct, balanced, fair laws to guide them. Laws not based upon the Word of God are always unfair, and are not Laws, since only God can institute and command a Law, but are merely imposter legalities, and restrictions, and limitations, which are arbitrarily imposed, by sinful mortal men, upon other mortal men, upon whom they can exert forced compliance.

The fourth listed gift of the Spirit is exhortation, and it is certain that the nation of Israel is the source and headwater of the stream of exhortation, including all the Holy prophets of God, that exhorted the people of Israel to return to true worship and obedience to God, and the Lord Himself (Who really, aggressively, confronted the wandering hearts of His people), and including all the Christians that followed after, preaching the gospel, and urging all people everywhere to return unto God.

The fifth listed promise unto Abraham is that God will bless those that bless Israel, and it has been proven time and again in the history of every single person and every single nation throughout the centuries. When the Greeks were friendly unto the Hebrews, the Greek culture and empire increased and expanded. The same phenomenon occurred when Rome later became an ally of Israel, and helped to defend the people of Israel from their former friends, the Greeks. Rome expanded, and increased. The same thing happened in more modern times, when England supported the cause of Israel, in the first half of the twentieth century. England rose to spectacular prominence on the world scene. The corresponding gift of the Spirit is giving, and the Lord has continually proven that to give something good unto Israel is to be guaranteed something good being given back later, with interest. God fulfills His promises, even if it sometimes takes a long time. He always balances His books.

The sixth promise God made to Abraham is that He would curse those that cursed the descendants of Abraham. The same nations used in the last illustration complete the example here. Once the Greeks began to war against Israel, the Greek nation and culture degenerated, and eventually was overcome. The same result was obtained by Rome, although it took a couple of more centuries, since Rome was after all, much vaster and stronger than Greece. Also, England fell from world leadership very soon after the English decided to hinder Israel and the fulfillment of its' national destiny, as foretold in the Holy prophets of God. The sixth gift of the Spirit is leadership, or authority, and God always faithfully proves that He is the real Authority over all the business of Israel, and all the other nations on earth, also. (Don't mess with Texas, of course. Do not even think about messing with Israel!)

The final promise that God made to Abraham is that in him all the families of the earth would be blessed. Already listed above are very many examples of some ways in which all the families of the earth have been blessed through Israel. The most powerful and significant is, of course, the Lord Jesus, Himself. He showed us all hope again, and knowledge of a future life, and how to actually live in peace with God, and our brothers and sisters, even here and now. He even taught us how to live in peace with ourselves, which is something no one else but Him could ever achieve. After all, He is the Prince of Peace, the King of Salem, High Priest forever, after the Order of Melchizedek. It seems magnificently appropriate that the seventh listed gift of the Spirit is showing mercy.

THE NON-CONFORMIST

Moses watched as the twelve men arrived before him, and he thought about each of them, and the tribe each man headed. The man he already knew best on a personal level was Joshua, and not just because Joshua was chief of the tribe of Ephraim. Ephraim was one of Joseph's sons that had been promoted to head his own new tribe, once the Lord had commanded that the tribe of Levi would no longer be numbered among the twelve tribes, but would be the sole proprietors of the priestly offices. Joshua was also Moses' personal assistant, and even remained at the Tent of Meeting continually, while Moses came and went back and forth to the Israelite camp, which was set at some distance apart from the Tent of Meeting.

Another man with whom Moses was closely familiar was Caleb, of the tribe of

Judah, who had often proven to be a courageous and brilliant military commander, with the ferocity and boldness of a true lion, and the always-smarter and never-defeated strategic genius that would be his trademark in war for all of his long, adventurous life. Caleb also was well known and respected as a man of flawless character. He lived out the law of God joyfully, and delighted in doing things God's way. Caleb was a practical, real world, clear-issue thinker, who regarded the ultimate reality as the actual existence of a very real, very aware, and very loving Heavenly Father.

Joshua was every bit as sincere a worshipper and follower of the Lord, but tended to have a more other-realm type of focus, and awareness, which suited him well, since he often saw and heard some very strange things, indeed, as Moses' personal assistant. Joshua was one of those, like his direct ancestor, Joseph, to whom the Lord had granted the gift to dream dreams, and see visions.

Moses gave them all their orders, precisely as the Lord had commanded him, and dispatched them to quietly enter the Promised Land, and to spy out everything about the land, including the forestation, terrain, cities and fortifications, and the inhabitants, and their preparedness for war. The men were to note every kind of information: locations, distances, and water sources, and even bring back some of the fruit of the new land to sample.

The spies were gone for forty days, and then returned from their mission. They did indeed bring back a huge cluster of grapes from the new land, and some other fresh fruits, as well. They reported that the land was indeed lush beyond their wildest dreams, but that it was already inhabited by six extraordinarily fierce nations, including many giants, distant descendants of evil demons that had defiled humanity with their corrupted DNA.

Ten of the spies scared the whole nation of Israel, with all their fearsome tales of ferocious man-eating giants, with sharp, pointed teeth, that constantly committed horrible atrocities upon anyone they happened to capture in battle, or in conquest. Even if those tales were not exaggerations, but literal truth, there were still two men that had also gone and also seen those things with their own eyes, and still waited a moment until the roar of protest had quieted a little bit.

Joshua remained silent, outwardly, but was praying intensely, inside. Caleb, moved suddenly by the Holy Spirit, shouted out so loudly that he drowned out all the hundreds of thousands of voices roaring their anger. As the entire nation fell to a stunned silence, Caleb spoke out in a crystal-clear voice, which carried all the way to the farthest person in the crowd. He urged the nation to stay trusting in God, and not to fear the terrible giants, but to know that God was with them, and they would not lose, even to giants. After Caleb paused a second for breath, like lightning, before the protestors could speak up, Joshua also raised his own powerful voice, and affirmed everything Caleb had just said to be true. Joshua also proclaimed that there was no reason to fear those little bitty giants, since the God of Israel was much larger than all of them put together.

This was too much for the protestors, so that in their cowardice and foolishness they began to shout for Caleb and Joshua to both be stoned.

That was too much for the Lord, Who immediately arrived in Person as the Glory of the Lord, and terrified all the crazy Israelites into silence before Him. He spoke, but only in the hearing of Moses, Caleb, and Joshua, and proclaimed that none of the evil Israelites that had complained and rebelled against the Lord would be allowed to enter the Promised Land, but that their bodies would die and rot in the wilderness. He specified by name that only Caleb and Joshua of all the Israelites there that day would live to actually enter the Promised Land. It is unknown exactly how that prophecy was understood by Moses, since his own name was not listed, but that is precisely how the Lord worked things out, around thirty-eight years later.

KING OF WARRIORS

Only a few short weeks had passed since the God of Israel had fulfilled His promise to bring His chosen people into their Promised Land. As he had done forty years earlier at the Gulf of Aquba in the Red Sea, once again the Lord had commanded the waters to part, and to remain parted, while His people, every one of them, walked safely across the dry ground to inherit the promise of God.

All of the local nations and their kings were shaking in fear of the Israelites. They had heard how God had stopped the mighty Jordan River, and had kept it stopped, while all the people walked through the dry riverbed which had been, for all of history, a nearly impassable torrent of powerful, noisy currents, that were so strong and swift in places that even men upon horses could be swept away and drowned, so suddenly that they could not even be heard to cry out for help before the Jordan had killed them.

The entire nation of Israel, men, women, children, and pets, was encamped only a couple of miles away from Jericho. The precise time had arrived for the Passover, and the Israelites worshipped, according to the command of God, and celebrated the feast with manna that the Lord was still providing for them from Heaven. The next day after the Passover was Sunday, and starting that same day, the Israelites ceased to eat manna, and instead began to eat the fruit of the Promised Land. They started out with unleavened bread, made from local grains, and also roasted whole grain and seeds.

Joshua and Caleb were deep in thought about the precise strategy they needed to plan to be able to destroy Jericho. It stood right smack dab in the middle of the region that Israel needed to control to be able to set up and maintain a practical, stable headquarters and fortress encampment, from which the army of Israel could continue its' conquest of the enemy nations already there. Caleb was back at camp, pouring over maps and sketches they had made of the entire Jericho area, including detailed drawings of the double walls that made this particular city so unbreakable. Joshua was too restless to stay in camp, and had a few of his best scouts with him, as they explored the far side of the city, looking for any chink in the armor. Jericho had a fresh water spring inside it, and also had stored up many hundreds of tons of dried grain and dried fruit, and also dried jerky and other strong meats for their fighting men. Jericho was prepared for a very long siege indeed, and was not about to send out any harassing sorties against Israel, since the rulers of Jericho knew the Israelites would never go away, of give up, and anyone sent out on such a raid would only be immediately caught and killed. After all, just a few weeks earlier, God had made the Jordan mind its' manners for them, so no one really thought they had any chance against both the Israelites and God as a team. They kept the gates locked, anyway, hoping the Israelites would eventually become uninterested, or maybe the other nations around would finally gather some courage, and some armies, and come to lift the siege off of Jericho.

As Joshua came over the rise of a small hill, he saw another slightly higher hilltop before him. Standing alone upon the very top of the hill was a large Man, dressed for serious warfare, and standing with His Sword drawn, and pointed straight at Joshua, as an unmistakable challenge. Joshua ordered his men to remain in place, while he drew his own sword, and with uncharacteristic trembling, determinedly and slowly walked forward until he was about twenty feet away from the strange Warrior.

Joshua cleared his throat nervously, and then said, as bravely as he could, "Are you for us, or against us?" For some reason he did not understand, something about this lone Soldier terrified him deep inside, even though Joshua was never afraid of a fight to the death, even against a giant, since he knew that the Lord was with him, and giants had no chance at all against the Holy Spirit.

The very large Man still had not moved even a single bit, and was utterly silent, until He suddenly replied, in a Voice that sounded like the roaring of a waterfall, "I am here before you as the Commander-in-Chief of the Army of Heaven!"

When He spoke the title "Commander-in-Chief" a strange and powerful thing happened. For a split second, Joshua, and his men, about fifty feet further away, all suddenly saw the King of Kings in His full Glory. They all fell to their faces, shaking in terror.

For almost two full minutes, no one moved or spoke. Joshua was the bravest fighter in all of Israel, and no man could stand before him in a fight, but it took all of his courage and strength to finally ask, as he trembled, "What does my Lord want His servant to do?"

The Son of God told him quietly to stand up, and He began to explain precisely how He wanted Joshua and all of Israel to conquer Jericho, and very specifically instructed him in what to do with all the inhabitants, and also all of the spoils of war they would soon acquire. Joshua memorized in great detail what His Lord commanded, and, when told to do so, turned and walked back to camp with his best scouts, and none of them spoke a word on the whole walk back, for over an hour.

The next morning, early, Joshua assembled all the whole congregation of

Israel, and passed along the precise orders he had been commanded. The Israelites prepared for battle, just as instructed. Then, for a whole week, they went out and did what they had been told. They marched around the closed-up city all the way, one time each for six days, with armed soldiers in front, followed by priests, blowing large trumpets made from ram's horns. The priests also carried the Ark of the Covenant with them. Following them were the armed soldiers which protected the rear of the very long column.

On the seventh day, at the very first light, the whole procession was up and at it again. This day, they completed seven entire circuits of the city, blowing the trumpets the whole time, which required several hours. The Lord had specified seven trumpets, a forward glimpse to the time of His return, and so there were plenty enough of the priests to change trumpeters whenever fatigue took it's toll.

Meanwhile, up in the sky overhead and all around Jericho, millions of God's angels had quietly, invisibly arrived and formed their ready-to-charge position. At the very pinnacle of the Army of Heaven, Tzedek-el, the General of the war-angels, stood in the air with his mighty wings extended, but motionless, as were the other angels. Next to him, also standing motionless upon the air, was another Person, the King of Kings, attired in His Royal Battle Armor. His Sword was not yet drawn, but His mighty Hand rested upon its hilt. As the Israelite Army, upon the ground, completed the final circuit of Jericho, Joshua ordered the people to shout when the priests all blew one very long, loud note upon the trumpets, and the King of Kings drew His mighty Sword, and a dazzling flash of light made everyone's eyes blind for a split second. Then the priests blew the long note, the

Israelites shouted, and the King of Kings, and the General, and all the other angels also shouted, and they suddenly flew, as fast as thought, straight down to places upon the walls of Jericho. There were so many angels that, as enormous as each angel was, there was just enough room all around the city walls, both inner and outer, so that the angels were shoulder-to-shoulder, with no gap anywhere. In less than a second, each angel had pulled down his section of the wall, every one at precisely the same moment, and the entire defensive wall system fell straight down, outward from the town. The people of Jericho were so terrified that they all fell into panic, and ran screaming toward the center of the city, clustering there, hoping to hide or escape. All the hopes of Jericho were in vain that special day, and not one living thing survived, except every man, woman, and child, and also the pets, of Israel. The good angels left unhurt, as did the General.

The King of Warriors also suffered no hurt that day. He would endure and conquer pain and humiliation like no other human ever experienced, and He would defeat it all by Himself, but that would not occur in time for another fourteen centuries, and then it would happen only because He willingly agreed to bear my punishment upon what was supposed to be my cross.

SWIFT JUSTICE

The whole thing started a short time after the last dark blue twilight faded out to complete black. There was no sight of moon or stars this cloudy night, and there were ominous rumblings in the distant sky, with occasional faint flashes of very high altitude lightning. The soldiers were in their tents for the night, except for the watches, and the animals were tethered securely for the night.

Suddenly, silently, and instantly lethally, the thousand or so watch sentries all fell quietly to the ground, dead. They did not fall precisely simultaneously, but each one died in rapid-fire sequence, one soldier at a time. The last one began to fall to the ground only about twenty seconds after the first sentry had been struck. A thousand sentries are very many, indeed, but not too many, when guarding the camp of an army that numbered almost two hundred thousand soldiers.

Over the course of the next hour, the execution continued at the same unyielding pace. If there had been any observers left alive to see, there might have seemed to be a lightning-like flicker of blue light, moving at impossible velocity, actually touching the heart of every one of the enemy soldiers the split second he was killed. It moved through the tents, trees, rocks, horses, campfires, and everything else as though they did not exist. It caused no harm at all to anything or anyone except the evil enemy soldiers, who had proven over the last several months to all have hearts of stone. Wherever they had conquered any town or nation, these Syrians, led by insane and proud Sennacherib, had committed horrible atrocities and extremely cruel destruction upon their helpless victims. They had no respect for anything civilized, and delighted in hurting others as much as they could, before the victim finally died. Their evil hearts were not hidden from the Lord, however, and He had just about had enough of them.

The final straw had been when the Syrian king had sent a message unto King Hezekiah, demanding absolutely barbaric terms, or utter destruction. King Hezekiah took the message, laid it down before the Lord, and prayed that Jerusalem would be spared the devastation that the Syrians were about to accomplish. The Lord heard, and answered "Yes!" to the prayer, and to the King who asked for it.

That answer arrived in the form of one of the Lord's favorite soldiers. The angel was named Tzedek-el, which means "Justice of God" and described him perfectly. He is the commanding General of the ground troops of the Army of Heaven, and had already fought many long wars and battles to help the Children of Israel escape complete annihilation.

He was especially chosen for this mission, since it was extremely unusual for the Lord to send His angels into direct combat against humans, even evil ones, since the outcome of the battle was always a human fatality. This time only one angel had been sent, since only one was needed.

The night was still a very hard one, even for a very mighty angel like the General, but he never grew tired. His heart hated having to kill anyone originally made in the image of his beloved God, but a larger part of his heart loved the Lord, and rejoiced to do His will, and this particular angel had been created with an unsurpassed delight in carrying out the Justice of God, and sometimes that meant killing the wicked. As he moved through the Syrian army, he clearly saw each man's wicked heart, and the horrible cruelties each one had constantly done. All he did was touch each wicked heart he saw that night, and force the truth inside that evil heart, and the shock of the man's own sin killed him immediately.

He did not linger with any particular one of them at all, nor did he look behind him to see how they fell. He had a mission to finish before daylight, and he would never fail, and he never had failed at anything. He did have to keep moving, however, since there were many hearts to be touched that night. He was moving at a rate human eyes would not have seen, anyway, since he was killing them at the rate of about fifty six of them every second. Every minute that passed, another three thousand enemy soldiers died. After an hour had passed, about one hundred eighty-five thousand enemy soldiers had died. The entire event was silent, except for the sound of dead men falling down, if they were the first watchmen that were killed, and all the others perishing in their beds, quietly. It was actually a humane execution, since the men did not have time enough to feel any pain, except a split second of crushing, true guilt for their evil.

A little over one hour and twelve minutes after the first death, it was all over. Not one person in the enemy camp whose heart was not wicked had been harmed at all. The General had followed the orders given to him by the Lord, and done so precisely, and left the evil Syrian king and his inner circle of hell-soldiers alive, but they would flee for their lives back to Syria in a few more hours, when daylight revealed that they suddenly had an army of dead men. Instead of being ready to fight, the Syrian army would be eaten by the birds. There were about one hundred and eighty five thousand fresh meals for the hungry birds.

The General stopped a moment, and for a second, looked over the dead enemy camp. His eyes saw one of the devil's soldiers, glaring at him from the other side of the camp. Tzedek-el stretched his huge neck: right, then left, and cracked all of his mighty knuckles, and laid his right hand on the hilt of his sword. Then he smiled a very grim smile at the enemy angel, one that he knew to be one of the highest ranking demons working for hell. The evil angel recoiled in sudden fear, and flew away from the camp instantly. The General smiled, this time a wide, genuine, happy smile, now that his mission was finished, and he flew back to Heaven until the next battle or war needed him.

INTO THE FIRE

The control freak of a king had decreed it, and his pride and reputation were at stake. The entire kingdom, and even the entire world, would be watching, to see if the mighty king would yield to the three Hebrew teenagers. They had declared in his court, before all of his nobles and men of power, that they would not bow down to the king, or his golden idol, even if he killed them for disobedience.

They refused to bow in most polite and respectful manners, but they still refused. They explained to the king that it was against their faith for them to bow before anyone but the God of Israel, no matter what.

Hananiah, Mishael, and Azariah were ready to live their lives for God, and they were ready also to give their lives for God. They prophesied that God could deliver them from the hand of the crazy

king, but that, even if He did not, they
still would not bow.

The king in his anger had his men heat
the idol and the furnace in its' evil belly
many times hotter than they had ever
heated it before. This was accomplished
by extra wood, and extra lamp oil and tar,
and several men standing near the door
into the furnace, fanning furiously with
large wooden paddles, producing a stiff
breeze, which acted like a giant bellows,
and accelerated the growth and intensity
of the fire. Some of these men were so
over heated that they died from thermal
shock. The ones closest to the fire were
the soldiers ordered to throw in the bound
and helpless teenagers. Not only did all
of those soldiers die quickly (also from
thermal shock), all of them also burst into
flames as they died, from the overload of
super-heat pouring out of the furnace,
like thick, invisible liquid fire.

The Babylonians were cold hearted
people. What other kind of monster,

except one with solid ice for a heart, could ever behave in such a fashion? To the observers, listening to the screams of the dying, and trying to make out all the gory details, the events actually inside the furnace were hard to discern. There was the small volcano of smoke, and the intense heat made all the air around the near vicinity of the idol shimmer with heat waves, distorting even ordinary things. There was also the chaotic thrashing about of the dying men, so the whole thing was difficult to clearly see from more than forty feet away, but any closer was unbearably hot, if one wanted to survive.

After a few minutes, all the men outside the oven had either died, or fallen back, or been dragged back, some still ablaze, by other survivors. They looked daggers at the evil king, but not one of them dared to say a word, knowing it could be his turn next.

Inside the furnace, strange things were happening. The Hebrew teenagers had felt the heat as they approached the fire, and had been singing Hebrew psalms of praise as they were carried to their deaths. They were scared, all right. Lesser men would have soiled themselves with that much fear. Somehow, they encouraged each other, and placed all hope in the God of Abraham, Isaac, and Jacob.

As they were thrown in, eyes shut tight, and hearts pounding like drums, suddenly the heat vanished, as though someone had closed a door. As they stood to their feet, they noticed that all of their ropes had burned completely away, in a flash, but their clothes, and even their hair, remained all thoroughly unhurt.

The brightness of the fire was still all around them, even though the heat was gone. As they blinked their eyes to adjust to the dazzle, and squinted to see, they saw a Man standing a few feet in front of them, right in the very center of the fire. The fire parted a space like a globe of normal air around Him, and He smiled at them as their eyes focused upon Him.

"Well done, mighty warriors! Your battle is over, now. You will be released in a few minutes, and promoted to positions of great power and influence in this kingdom, and will, for many years, lead many away from death, and into truth. Excellent servants of the true King, indeed!"

As soon as they had seen Him, the boys had all bowed low to the ground, and listened, trembling, to what He said. As He paused for a moment, the oldest, Hananiah, asked Him "What is Your Name?"

He waited another few seconds until all of the boys were looking Him in the eye. Then He smiled again, and said, "Melchizedek."

SHUT UP, AND GET OUT OF MY CHURCH!

It was right after He had been rejected by the folks He had grown up among. The proud hotheads in Nazareth had stirred up the crowd over an imagined insult, when all He had actually done was to tell them the truth. It was not a very flattering truth about them, and they reacted with intent to actually kill Him. He had simply walked through another dimension of space and time, and passed right through the middle of them, and quietly, invisibly, gone His way.

Now, He was at Capernaum, and He was invited to be guest speaker, or visiting preacher, at the worship services on Saturday. As soon as He had moved to the place up front, a demon-possessed man stood up, shaking his fist at Jesus, and shouted for Jesus to let everyone alone, and that he knew Who Jesus was, the Holy One of God. Jesus calmly told the evil spirit to shut up and leave. The demon threw the man about fifteen feet into the middle of the room, but was instantly gone, and the man, blinking his eyes, and rubbing his shoulder, where he had landed, seemed pretty much all right.

Jesus was not about to tolerate a heckler from the devil in His worship service that day. When He had healed the man, everyone locked attention on every move He made, and engraved every Word He said into their memories. They had never seen anyone else just order the evil spirits around like that, and then get to watch them instantly obey.
One of the biggest reasons He ordered them to shut up is that it is not His will that people should find salvation from the words of demons. They work for the father of lies, and lies do not save anyone.

After the services, He went to Peter's house for lunch, but Peter's mother in law was sick with a fever. He stood by her, and ordered the fever to leave, and within ten minutes, after a cup of water, the lady was feeling so much restored that she insisted on getting up and making them all dinner, with her daughter's help. They decided to let her, since stubbornness was common with everyone in Peter's family, a characteristic that the Lord later would use to make them unbreakable in their faith.

Around sundown, the people from all the small towns and countryside around there came to see Him, and He healed everyone who needed it. He kicked out more evil spirits as well. Many people were restored that day and evening, all because He had knowingly allowed a demon-possessed man to sneak into the synagogue. Even so, He had immediately kicked the demon out, and let the man stay. Not only that man, but every one else around there was eager to hear and obey a Man that could do all those wonderful things.

Still, it does make one wonder. If, in the time of Jesus, in the land of Israel, on a Sabbath, in a Jewish synagogue, and when the guest preacher for the day, for crying out loud, is JESUS, HIMSELF, then how does a person with an evil spirit inside them even get near the place? Maybe not everyone that goes to church every Sunday in our own times is completely clean from evil spirits, either. More important than the worshipper being inside a church is that the King of all churches is inside of the worshipper.

MEN LIKE TREES, WALKING

Psalm 1

1 Blessed *is* the man that walketh not in the counsel of the
    ungodly, nor standeth in the way of sinners, nor sitteth
    in the seat of the scornful.
2 But his delight *is* in the law of the LORD; and in his law
    doth he meditate day and night.
3   And he shall be like a tree planted by the rivers of
water, that bringeth forth his fruit in his season; his leaf also
shall not wither; and whatsoever he doeth shall prosper.

Genesis 49:
22Joseph *is* a fruitful bough, *even* a fruitful bough by a well;
whose branches run over the wall:

The Lord Jesus and His disciples were
entering Bethsaida, the hometown of two
of His earliest followers, Philip, and
Nathaniel. All of them had been very
busy at the Sea of Galilee, where for
three non-stop days of preaching,
teaching, and healing, over four thousand
men, plus women and children, too, had
listened intently, trying to hear,

understand, and remember every magnificent Word and Deed they had seen this modern-day Prophet proclaim and perform. He had stunned them all into amazement, showing them many things that had been almost forgotten since the centuries before, when earlier prophets had foretold them. He told them about the Kingdom of Heaven, in ways they could understand. He used simple, easy to remember stories of people who had in some way illustrated the point He was communicating. Only the Person Who had witnessed everything in history, since before the world began, would know and remember the precise, perfect, true historical event or story which could now enable the ordinary people, and even the children, to grasp and retain the main ideas that He needed to share with them. He spoke deep Words that penetrated to the very core of one's awareness, and stuck in the heart, Words that were welcomed by those who loved Him, and resented, because of their own guilt, by those who hated Him.

That was not all. To prove He was precisely Who He claimed to be, He also did more miracles every hour than they could count. The whole time, as He proclaimed the Good News of the Kingdom of Heaven, He also was walking among them all, continually touching, blessing, and healing every person in the crowd. A few people were scared of Him when He drew near, but after they looked into His infinitely wise Eyes, and felt His warm, strong touch, their fear melted, and a thrill of joy they had never known in their lives shot into them like a lightning bolt. They often smiled and laughed quietly, but some wept tears of pure joy and relief. He healed not only their broken bodies, but also their tormented minds and hearts. As for the evil angels He saw trying to hide from Him inside some of their hearts, He snarled viciously at them, as He ordered them, as they screamed, to vacate at once! He did not have to shout. All the while, He spoke in a normal tone of voice, but everyone in the whole crowd could hear every single Word clearly.

As sundown had approached on the third day, He told the disciples to feed them with the seven loaves, and a few small fish, that were the raw material from which He miraculously brought forth a bountiful supply, enough to feed them all, and much left over. He told them to gather up he fragments that remained, which totaled seven large baskets full, more than the original amount by far, and symbolized the fulfillment of the seven-fold Spirit of God and the completed Kingdom. The reason He had told them to be sure that "nothing is lost" is because He will not leave behind even one soul that He can possibly save from the lake of fire. Every member of the population of all the saints, from the Resurrected, will certainly qualify as someone who was once a broken fragment, and a leftover, also.

When they had arrived in the center of the town, a small crowd of local folks had gathered, and brought Him a man who was blind, and wanted to be healed. The Lord looked into the man's heart, and saw a humble and obedient child of light, who had just lived a very hard life, and been often taken advantage of by selfish people, who had only wanted to gain from his good natured generosity. Now times had been very hard for him, since his eyesight had failed, and he could no longer work. The Lord also looked at the people in the small crowd, and saw in their hearts the selfishness which they had used as a weapon of destruction against this man, their own blood kin, since he had been a young boy. He had never stopped trying to give goodness unto others, no matter how little he himself had, and others had lazily taken away and used up everything he ever had, until he himself was squeezed bone dry, and they still wanted their easy touch back again. The Lord had compassion on the kind-hearted blind man, but was angry with his no-good relatives.

The Lord commanded the townsfolk not to follow them out of the town, in a very stern tone, that no human being ever created could have the strength to disobey. He and the twelve quietly led the blind man out of town about a mile, well out of sight of the people there. The Lord Jesus stopped, turned the man to face Him, and said, "Receive your sight!" Then He spit once upon each of the man's closed eyes, as He held him by his shoulders, so he would not fall down or lose his balance. The man blinked several times, and rubbed his eyes dry with his hands.

The Lord asked him what he saw. The man answered, "I see men like trees, walking."

The Lord told him to close his eyes again, and He touched the man's eyes again, and told him to look up. This time the man could see everyone the same way he had before anything happened to his eyesight.

He smiled and fell to his knees, praising God. Jesus lifted him up, and said, "You did not do anything wrong, except allow others to trample your pearls underfoot, then turn and destroy you, like the swine they are. Forsake the foolish, and live, and go in the way of understanding. Leave this town, or your selfish relatives will hear of you restoration, and try to get you to pay all of their bills again, forever. Go, start a new life, wherever God leads you, and do whatever He tells you to do. Only, do not do it here any more."

As the man obediently turned, right then, to walk away forever from his lifetime hometown, one of the disciples asked the Lord why He had not healed the man fully the first try. Jesus smiled, and said, "Peter, you did not correctly understand what happened. The first time, his eyes were opened so that he saw people as they appear in the Spirit's realm, where folks appear as living, moving fruit trees, some of which bear good fruit, and some of which bear bad fruit. You will know what kind of tree a person is by what kind of fruit his life produces. A good tree can only produce good fruit, and a bad tree can only produce bad fruit. Stay away from bad trees, their fruit is poisonous."

SINS OF THE FATHERS

Thomas heard a slight sound on the road behind them. Of all the disciples, only Thomas, and Simon the Zealot, and Judas the son of Simon had ever actually been military soldiers. They all three tended to stay at the outer edges of the group of disciples, and Thomas in particular always chose the rear guard position. He was the most trained and veteran soldier of all of them, and had once been part of the elite Temple Guard, respected as the finest and toughest of all the soldiers in Israel. They lived and died to honor their nation, and followed in the noble tradition of warriors like Joshua and Caleb, and David, and David's special operations troops, six hundred of the bravest and most deadly fighters who ever went into battle, with faces like lions, and hearts to match.

Thomas turned and instantly relaxed, when he saw a single person running down the road after them. Even though Thomas had resigned from the Temple guard, having become disgusted with the open hypocrisy and hidden corruption that saturated the whole place, he still took his soldier's calling very seriously, and was always ready to fight to defend the others, as well as his own life. He had learned to wait a bit and watch, however, as time and again, the Master had somehow miraculously diffused and extinguished an explosive moment. He was still always ready, but had learned to be ready to wait, as well as ready to fight. As soon as he looked at Jesus, and opened his mouth to say, "Master!" the Lord immediately answered him, as He stopped walking, and before He turned around, "Yes, Thomas, thank you. I see him, too." As He said this, Jesus turned around, smiled at Thomas, and looked intently at the approaching lone man. The

Lord's brow tensed as He stared deep into the man, though he was still almost a hundred yards away, then Jesus smiled a bit, as though recognizing someone He had known a very long time ago, but had lost from contact over time.

The young man came up, gasping for breath, and did not bow before Jesus, but sort of held up one hand in a sort of timid wave, with a rather uncertain little smile. "Good Master, what good thing must I do, so that I may inherit eternal life?"

Jesus smiled broadly, as though at some obvious but still private joke, and said, "Why are you calling Me good? There is One Who is good, God."

Jesus continued, "But if you want to have eternal life, keep the commandments."

The young fellow answered, "Which ones?"

In reply, Jesus began to list several of the primary ten commands listed on the Two Tablets, but not in their normal order. The first one He quoted was, "Thou shalt not commit adultery, thou shalt not murder, etc."

The young man answered again, "All of these I have kept from my youth."

Then the Lord looked very, very deeply into his heart, and saw that which pleased Him much, that this young man, centuries downstream from his greedy, materialistic ancestors, actually had a heart that loved God, and wanted to do goodness to help others in honor of God's goodness. He smiled gently at the young man, and said, "One thing you still lack. Sell everything you have, and give to the poor, and you will have treasure in Heaven."

The young man looked stunned at the words, and then quietly turned, and slowly walked back up the road, back to where he started. He walked with his head hung down, lost in thought, wondering how he could ever give up all his family wealth, which had been increasing for hundreds of years.

A few days later, Jesus and His followers were just nearing Jericho, and, near the outer edge of the town, a blind man, the son of Timaeus, sat begging for alms by the roadside. As he heard increasing noise and commotion when Jesus began to draw near, he suddenly realized just Who this was approaching, and he began to cry out desperately, at the top of his lungs, "Son of David, have mercy on me!" He kept on doing it, too, even when those folks nearby him shouted at him to shut up.

Jesus heard him, and said, "Bring him here!"

Suddenly the protesting, angry people, that less than two minutes before had been yelling at Bar-Timaeus to shut up, had instantly all become his best buddies, saying, "Cheer up, He's calling for you!"

When Bar-Timaeus arrived, escorted by the former soldier Thomas, and another combat veteran, Simon, he immediately fell on his knees before Jesus, and asked that he might just be given his sight once more. Jesus healed him, and the man leaped and danced wildly around, absolutely delighted to be able to see everything and everyone clearly again! He came back, fell before Jesus again, and thanked Him over and over. Jesus lifted him up and said, "Your faith has made you whole."

Jesus watched Bar-Timaeus walk away down the road, going home to tell all his family the wonderful news. Only the Lord understood that the two men with which He had just had such interesting events had much more in common than they realized. Centuries before, the ancestor of Bar-Timaeus, a man named Lazarus, who had been separated from his wife and children by war and sickness, but had never stopped loving them, had waited day and night outside the locked gates of the rich, heartless ancestor of the rich young man. The rich young man had gone away empty. Bar-Timaeus had received his sight, and a new life again. The rich young man did indeed love God, but he also loved his riches. That was why the Lord had listed adultery as the first warning to the young man. Through the centuries, the rich man's family had bound themselves to riches and power, and had, in effect, emotionally married money, instead of uniting with God, and loving Him. So, the Lord gave the young man a clear choice. Love God, or love money. He could not serve both masters. The young man had chosen money, and walked away, sadly.

Lazarus and his family had always chosen God, and faith and obedience to Him. Many times such loyalty had cost them dearly, but the Lord always, somehow, eventually made it all up to them, in the end. True, some of them had to die first to inherit their riches, but every one of them finally did, and in a place where they would never be poor again.

MADE IN HIS IMAGE

When the Lord commanded all of reality to "Let Us make man in Our Own image!" it was not a suggestion, or the spoken stray thought of our Creator to relieve His boredom with a new hobby. He meant it as a direct order, and nothing in existence is allowed to violate that order, upon pain of death in the lake of fire.

This project is the central reason that the Maker made anything else at all, beside His Own complete Life, without need for anyone else. He wanted Children of Light, since He is the Father of Lights. He created energy, time, space, and matter, so He could build physical human bodies: living, breathing, real people. He designed and built the entire universe, and everything in it, seen or unseen, known to man, or unknown to man, and

He balanced everything so flawlessly that the whole blessed thing works!

He displays His limitless wisdom and knowledge and power by designing, building, and maintaining all things, from the sub-atomic, and the tiny little natural nano-bots and micro-machines within the living cell, all the way up to and including clusters and superclusters of galaxies, structures so vast and massive that the human mind cannot comprehend them.

As if that were not impressive enough, far beyond the form is the function, including living creatures, with solid bodies assembled from dust and mud, and, even more wonderfully, a living soul within each creature. Science can measure things, and count things, and calculate things, but it cannot explain why. If you want to know why, you must seek knowledge from God. He knows why He built everything the way that He did. Ask Him to open your understanding, and start doing your part, and study!

God is long-distance, full-spectrum, wide-angle, telephoto, huge, tiny, and every extreme limit and far beyond. You cannot put God in a box. He will not stay in there. The Son of God proved that when He came out of His tomb.

So, given how vast God is, and how terrifyingly, microscopically small and weak we are, precisely how is that called us being made in His mighty image?

A part of the answer may hide in the scripture that says that God has set eternity in the hearts of men. Every man who ever lived wanted to live forever, unless in extreme pain. The only reason a person ever wants to die is if they have lost hope, and the agony of their life becomes unendurable, so that even death seems a better choice. Still, what they really want is not to die, but to end the pain.

Jesus certainly was not suicidal, and did not want to die, but He wanted to end the pain, the pain of evil, and the sin and death that it produced in His little brothers and sisters (you and me). It was never His Own pain or death that He wanted, but His loving heart was strong enough to bear it for us. If love had not been His purpose and His motive, He could never have sincerely prayed for the Father to forgive us because we did not realize what we were doing, and also to forgive us for not knowing.

There is perhaps another way in which we are made in His image. When we love sincerely, and unselfishly, and when we forgive others who do us wrong, and release the offence unto the Lord, that is doing precisely as we were commanded by Him, that we love one another, as He loved us. He said that no one had greater love than this: that he would lay down his life for his friends. He said that we are His friends, if we do as He commanded us. When we lay down our anger (since the wrath of man works not the righteousness of God) then, with the help of the Holy Spirit, we are confirming that we are children of Light, who seek to obey our Big Brother, Jesus. After all, our Father has put Him in charge of running all of Heaven and earth.

A different perspective on the image concept is that man is defined by Jesus as a three part creature, comprised of the overlapping and intersecting components of body, mind, and heart. The combination of mind and heart is labeled soul. Those who are born again have new bodies, minds, and hearts, reborn of the Holy Spirit, through the Word of God. The heart begins to believe different things about God, and reality, and from the heart arise new thoughts in the mind, and as the heart is changing, and the thoughts in the mind are changing, and the words and the deeds that are said and done are changing, toward a new and cleaner life, the body's strength will often improve as well. Many times the recovery and improvement could accurately be described as miraculous.

We can also see a triple layer parallel structure between God and mankind in that the Father, Who made all of Heaven and earth, and everything and everyone everywhere, seems to correspond to the mind of man, and He relates to us through reason. He said for us to come, and reason together with Him.

The Holy Spirit corresponds to the heart of man, as He dwells within the reborn, and changes the things within our hearts, where no one but Him can heal us. He also first contacts the sinner to convict the lost one of his own sin, and his desperate need for rescue, which only is available through Jesus.

Jesus corresponds to the body of man, not only because He also has a human body, but He used the healing and repair of wounded and damaged bodies as one of His primary witnessing tools, so that people could actually feel in their bodies that the healing power of a wonderful and loving God was very real indeed.

Eternity is longer, stronger, and vastly more powerful than time. Eternity was before time, and is continuing all during the entire lifespan of time, and will still be around after time has ended.

Love is longer, stronger, and vastly more powerful than hate. Love was alive before hate ever existed, and is continuing all during the entire lifespan of hate, and will still be around after hate has ended.

The Father fills our minds with reason, and the Holy Spirit fills our hearts with love and eternity. Jesus will fulfill His promise, and raise us up in perfect bodies, just like His, at the Day appointed before the world began. From that Day on, forever (literally), there will be absolutely no doubt that He made us in His image!

THE WIND OF CHANGE

There was an evening during the week of Passover that a member of the Sanhedrin came secretly after nightfall to speak with Jesus. The man's name was Nicodemus, and he was the Chief Scribe of Israel. He personally did accept Jesus as God-in-the-flesh, but also had a very prominent and highly paid position on the Sanhedrin. If his visit to Jesus was discovered, he most certainly would have been kicked off of the Council, and fired from his career.

Jesus told him of many aspects of the Kingdom of Heaven, and also used some accurate parallel examples from the natural world to more precisely imprint the correct picture into the mind and heart of Nicodemus. One of the most mysterious and striking metaphors was that the wind blows where it wants to, but we cannot tell where it came from, or where it is going. Then Jesus said that is how it is with everyone who is born again of the Holy Spirit.

Nicodemus was confused about being born a second time, and asked how these things could be. Jesus observed that Nicodemus was the primary scripture teacher to all of Israel, including the Sanhedrin, and wondered how it was that he was unable to understand. Jesus commented that if told of earthly things, and even unable to understand those things, how would folks understand the things of Heaven?

At another time, Jesus was trying to reason with the scribes and Pharisees, and He told them that He knew where He came from, and where He was going, but they did not. Since Jesus and the Holy Spirit are One, He was precisely identifying Himself as similar in manner to the wind. It is unknown by mankind whether or not the wind is aware of anything at all, including where it came from, and where it goes. It is absolutely unquestionable that Jesus knew where He came from, and where He would be going.

During the final supper on Thursday night with His followers, at the Feast of the Passover, Jesus told them that He had come from God, and was going to God. He told them that if they loved Him they would rejoice, because His Father was greater than He was. He also assured them that, if He went away, He would come back and see them again, which He did, after death and resurrection. He also promised them that when He had ascended again to Heaven, to the Father, He would send the Holy Spirit to join up and stay with each of the born-again for the remainder of the believer's life, guiding the follower home safely to Jesus. He also faithfully keeps that promise, and the Spirit arrives first, even before the person believes, and the Spirit convicts the person of sin, of righteousness, and of judgment. The person who accepts the correction of the Holy Spirit is then granted a brand-new life in Jesus, and is then indwelt by the Lord Holy Spirit, and sealed and protected forever as one of the re-born of God. This entire process is a free gift from God, the person does not earn it, or deserve it, but God is both merciful, to forgive our sin, and gracious, to grant us Himself within our hearts, minds, and bodies. Anyone who is re-born is never alone.

The first thing that Jesus told everyone when He finished His test in the wilderness, after the angels came and ministered unto Him, (no, they did not preach to Him, or tell Him to send in donations to some televangelist; instead, they gave Him food and water, and helped to heal His exhaustion from His ordeal) was simply "Change!" The entire universe immediately began to obey and to change, and the changes have been spreading and accelerating ever since. There was a very visible example of this change to obedience He commanded, and enforced, when He once told the boisterous wind and water to shut up, and settle down, and everything instantly obeyed. The only "decision for Jesus" any human being can ever possibly make, on his own, is whether or not he is going to obey Jesus, if, by the grace of God, and ONLY by the grace of God, the person was privileged enough to be allowed to become a believer in the first place. No one can choose to believe, because God told us that we did not choose Him, but He chose us. All we can choose is whether or not we obey what He tells us.

So, in summary, the Wind of Change is Jesus. The change He commands is obedience. That Wind of Change is irresistible, and unstoppable, since He is the Wind blown into the world by the Breath of Almighty God. God has also promised us that His Word will never return to Him void, and that the scripture cannot be broken. God will finish what He started, and He will use the Wind of Change to accomplish it.

That was precisely what happened in the upper room where one hundred and twenty disciples were gathered, and there came the sound, as of a mighty rushing wind from Heaven, and there appeared something like tongues of fire upon the disciples, and they spoke with new tongues, after the Wind of Change had blown through and changed them all.

It is recorded in the scriptures that God will scatter the wicked with a blast of His Breath when He comes to judge. That will be the final time the Wind of Change will have to blast a change into creation, since, after He has removed the wicked, the grandest changes will stay accomplished forever.

WIND WALKERS

The wind blows where it will, but we
can't fathom it still.

We do not know where it began; its' path
is not seen by man.

Those re-born in the Spirit must live just
like the wind:
Driven there against the enemy, or here
to help a friend.

The Great Wind which moves us is just
the breath of God,
But the Pathway of the Wind is to be
walked all unshod.

We must walk by faith, is just what we
are told;
And we can walk upon that Wind, if our
faith is bold.

THE SIN OF IGNORANCE

When the time came that the disciples asked Jesus when would He return, and what would be the sign of His arrival, He began with the command to not allow anyone to deceive them. He then went on to list some very specific events that were yet to occur in the future. Since that day, some of those events have occurred, but some have still not.

Jesus also cautioned His followers to avoid the religious hypocrites, calling them blind guides of the blind. In proverbs the command is given to forsake the foolish, and live, and go in the way of understanding.

Just before He died on the cross, He prayed out loud that God would forgive us, for we knew not what we did. There is a double edge to that sword of His prayer. One the one edge, He asked God to forgive an offense done in ignorance.

On the other edge, He asked God to forgive us for being so damn ignorant.

Even though no one can receive anything, unless it is given to him from above, it is still our responsibility to seek God, and to study His Word, and to learn His Way, and to follow Him. We must pray for the Holy Spirit to open our hearts and minds, to know, and understand, and hear, and obey, all the things of God. It is the most difficult subject matter to study that does exist, but it is also the very most rewarding and fascinating. God and His Word are One, so when we study His word, we are studying Him.

MORTAL WOUND

It was, without question, the most unique and effective counter attack ever formulated. It did indeed work, and vastly more effectively than anyone except the Master Strategist had foreseen. The unstoppable and effective strategy of a sort of mammoth judo flip, in spiritual terms, had permanently broken the enemy, and divided the empire of evil against itself, so it could no longer stand, but began that moment to crumble down into fragments, like the Tower of Babel had once shattered and fallen into splinters.

The solution was the most costly price ever paid, also, since it cost God as Father His Only Begotten Son, and it cost the Son of God His humiliation, suffering, and tortured death, and it cost the Holy Spirit of God to have to come down here to all believers, and love and re-conceive them, with a spirit reborn of His Own Spirit.

Since the Day of Resurrection, it has also cost millions of followers of the Son of God much loss, persecution, rejection, abuse, suffering, and tortured death. It has also been continuing to cost the Holy Spirit to sustain us each one as we fight our way, His Way, through and out of the Valley of the Shadow of Death. It has continued to cost the Son of God, to have to watch, until the Day appointed, as those of us who love Him try to walk quietly the hard path, to pray sincerely for our enemies, even if we would rather punch them in the nose, and to forgive, from the heart, wrongs done not only to ourselves, but even to those we love. Our Heavenly Big Brother does not like it much when evil creatures try to hurt His little brothers or sisters. Some Day, they will all answer to Him.

This particular day was the cold day early in spring of 33 A.D., and the greatest Warrior to ever live was struggling all alone, hand to hand, in a bitter knife fight to the death against the whole empire of evil. Even though He was being unjustly punished for all the sin of all the people who ever would be saved, He still took it, not just like a man, but like a King. Perhaps many other strong men could have endured the agony, even the shame, and retained some tiny measure of self-control and dignity all the way until death. No one else that ever lived could have done it the way that He did it. He did win the war against evil, and utterly destroy the whole gross empire that day. He did it with class, not wasting His Words, or His last few precious breaths. He was recorded to have said several things before He died.

The significance of one or two of His last Words bears a closer look. We know He said "Paid in full!" We are certain that statement is His Royal Proclamation (even still King of Kings, and Lord of

Lords, even while dying upon the Cross) that all sin debt is forever cancelled, through His Own death, and that Royal Proclamation has all the full weight of the Law of God solidifying it, and is just as binding as the Law of Gravity.

We also know that He said, "Father, forgive them, for they know not what they do." We know that we are supposed to walk as He Himself also walked, and forgive those that wrong us. We know that we are to give place to wrath, for the wrath of man works not the righteousness of God. This is the main model for the Christian to follow, sincerely, from the heart, and we were warned, that if we do not forgive our troublemakers, God will not forgive us.

Perhaps, at the very moment He said, "Father, forgive them," a horrible shriek was heard from deep within the earth. At that precise second, the enemy's stone heart was cut in two, from top to bottom. As the people around the foot of the

Cross were hearing a great Blessing, the enemy felt the instant impact of the Sword that went out as the Word of Jesus. The moment that Royal Proclamation (expressed as the Prayer of the Son of God, for an example of what we should say in battle) was uttered, the stranglehold the devil had held upon earth was suddenly broken forever. The overwhelming power of Love in the Person of the Son of God had gently and instantly ripped all the captives of sin from hell, and at the same moment, violently torn the devil and hell right down the middle.

In the strange, quiet moment beneath a nearly pitch dark sky, when for a space, even all the terrible thundering had paused, the King gathered His final strength, and, with unimaginable agony, forced Himself to inhale one final breath. It was reported that after He said everything else, He shouted one final great shout, and died. The innocent King died unjustly, but willingly, to pay for you and me, and He also killed every bit of the power of evil forever, since it had been based upon sin, and sin died that day with our King.

We were not told precisely what it was that our King shouted with His very last breath, but I do not believe that He wasted it with a meaningless groan of pain. He had borne His torture and death all the way without even a sound, or a whimper. No, He surely must have said something very important. Maybe the reason the Words were not translated by the eyewitnesses was because it could have been from a language far more ancient than Aramaic, or Hebrew. Perhaps it was the ancient, Holy, Sacred, and secret Name of the Father, which all the Hebrew people were forbidden to speak in public, upon pain of immediate death. Even though we do not know the precise Word, we know it means "I AM THAT I AM" as well as "Justice!"

It also could have been the ancient language equivalent of "Mission accomplished! Threat eliminated!"

A NIGHT IN CHAINS

The latest offences the monster had committed were very typical of his mad behavior. He had always been the personification of a control freak. He was totally unable to control his own emotions, or his own actions, so he tried to manipulate or force everyone else around him to submit to his every whim. He ruled by brutality, and fear. He was not even of the same nation that he ruled over so cruelly. He was not, and never became, an Israelite. He was, in fact, an Edomite. If Rome had not forcibly placed him upon the throne in Jerusalem, he would never have become king.

He was just as ruthless and crazy as his sire had been. No matter which of the men named Herod was under discussion, in whatever year one of them was in power, it usually involved very bad news.

Peter was falling asleep in his cell, fairly certain that in the morning, the first day after the Passover, Herod would put him to death. It was the seven year anniversary of that special Sunday morning when Jesus had risen. Peter was actually sort of looking forward to it, except for, of course, the pain and dying parts. He certainly wanted to go be with Jesus again, and now James, the brother of John, was already there, too. Herod had just killed James a few weeks ago. Christians, made bold by the Holy Spirit, sometimes have unshakeable courage, to confront lies, and challenge evil face to face. James was still one of the sons of thunder, even though he was also now a re-born son of God. It is not impossible that James confronted Herod about the murder of John the Baptist, eight years earlier, and also about conspiring with the Sanhedrin and Pilate to have Jesus executed by the Romans. Whatever the provocation, James was gone, and Peter was next.

Instead of spending his last few moments awake in worry, Peter asked the Lord to help him make it through whatever was ahead. He then turned his attention in prayer to the protection and guidance of John. The boy was still reeling from the murder of his older brother, and losing Peter, too, was going to make it even tougher for him. He had grown into a fine, smart, tough young adult, and was constantly led by the Holy Spirit. When they had come to arrest Peter, John had just barely been persuaded to leave, and escape, but he respected Peter, and did follow orders from him to run. He would go hide among his family members, down by the Sea of Galilee. After a while, the boy would relocate to Ephesus.

Sometime deep in the night, Peter awoke to a bright light shining in his cell. He blinked his eyes, squinted, then made out an angel as the source of the bright light. He thought he was dreaming, and started to close his eyes again. Suddenly, a sharp smack to his ribs had Peter wide awake, and halfway to his feet. The angel told him to get on his clothes, and follow. The chains dropped off of his hands and feet, with a very loud clank when they hit the floor. Even so, the guards on either side of him did not even stir, except they kept breathing. Later, those same guards would come to wish that they had stopped breathing before daylight.

As Peter followed the angel out of the cell, the cell door, and every single door and barrier, opened silently in front of them, and then quietly closed behind them after they were through. The light from the angel still shone dazzlingly bright, but no one but Peter seemed to see him.

As soon as they had completely left the prison compound, and gone down one street, about two blocks long, they turned a corner, and the angel vanished, leaving Peter blinking at the glowing after-image, as his eyes adjusted to the night. Peter went from there to tell the other apostles that their prayers in his behalf had been answered, and it was not his ghost, but the real, live, flesh and blood Peter they all knew and loved. They were all astonished and delighted.

The angel had returned to the side of his General, Tzedek-el, less than one second after he had vanished from Peter. The General, along with a large portion of his main army, was hovering in the night air over Jerusalem. They had not brought the chariots, siege engines, or any of the flaming horses with them this time. They all had their swords already drawn, and were staring down at the evil angels that surrounded Jerusalem that night. The good angels were not daring the evil ones to try anything against Peter. They were just ready, if they did.

"Well done. Just keep an eye on him for tonight. The rest of us will suppress any interference."

The littlest angel smiled, and immediately returned to Peter, this time hiding his glow. He was happy to know that the General had trusted him to do such an important mission.

The two guards who had been in the cell from which Peter had escaped had a horrible morning, and a terrible last few hours in this world. The night before, they had cruelly mocked Peter, saying horrible things about Jesus, and how they were going to love watching Peter die slowly, while he screamed. Even though they never knew it, Peter had quietly prayed that, if possible, the Lord would forgive, and also save them, too.

Those men were hardened soldiers. They also knew they had not let Peter escape. Something supernatural must have occurred. As Herod had them tortured for hours the next day, perhaps the Lord worked a miracle, and answered Peter's prayer. Maybe those hardened soldiers at the very end had their hearts soften enough to accept the reality of Jesus as the Son of God. If they are seen some day in the streets of Heaven, the glory will go to God.

DAMASCUS

Even though it was a little after three in the morning, the strong old man walked steadily through the pitch black night. The streets of Damascus were almost empty, though there were every night some folks out and about that had crooked hearts, and who went out in the dark to commit their crimes and get away unseen before dawn. He did not fear them, because he knew that he was guarded, everywhere he went in this world.

The extreme darkness did not trouble him at all. The man had been given the most unusual sight abilities, and was able to see, directly, or somehow sense, very precisely, just what was where, and perceive the true inner nature of whatever he was looking upon. This applied especially to people, but also included animals, and even many things beyond the curtains which limit normal human perception.

As he turned into the street called Straight, two thieves rushed at him from the shadows. He saw their hearts, and immediately, with the strength he had used in much hard work all his life, and with a supernatural speed, quicker than the blink of an eye, he knocked them both unconscious, careful to not cause permanent damage, and then caught both of them, one with each hand, and lowered them gently to the street, so they would not be needlessly hurt in the fall. With a smile, and a whispered prayer for each of them, he resumed his journey. After all, they were just teenagers, and he had instantly seen that they, also, someday soon, would love and follow Jesus.

A few more blocks brought him to the gate of the house he had been sent to find. He pounded at the entry, and when the gatekeepers came, he told them who he was, and who he was there to see.

They opened up for him at once, and he
was escorted into the main house, and led
down a long passageway into a small
bedroom. As soon as he walked in, he
saw a man seated on a chair in the corner,
where he had been facing out the open
window. The man's face turned toward
them as they walked in. The large visitor
gasped at what he saw. In his mind he
saw a stump left of a once mighty tree.
The thing had been enormous, but now
all that remained was a broken, burned,
split, and shattered trunk, with all the
limbs broken off. Some of the broken
limbs could be seen lying around the
withered and ruptured roots of the thing,
and some of the poisonous, evil fruit was
still clinging uselessly to the broken
branches. It was horrible to see, a thing
that had been made to do goodness, but
had spent its' whole life doing terrible
evil, and all the while delighting to do it.

As he looked a little closer, once the
first shock had abated, he also noticed a

few new green sprouts, coming from deep within the old tree trunk, and the new growth was wholesome and strong, and wherever it passed through the old trunk into the air, it seemed that new, healthy growth was also being started in the old trunk, and the burned old bark was turning new, vital, and alive once again, but this time with wholesome goodness. The change had already begun.

The man walked over to the seated fellow, reached out his large, strong hands, gently held the smaller man with one hand on his shoulder, and one hand resting upon the top of his head, and firmly said, "Brother Saul, the Lord Jesus, Who appeared to you on the road as you traveled, has sent me that you may receive your sight, and be filled with the Holy Spirit!"

As he said this, something like a brief but powerful electric shock passed through both of them from the top of their heads down throughout their whole bodies, but with only power, and healing, and clean strength, and no trace of pain. Something like fish scales fell from Saul's eyes to the floor, and he began to blink and rub his eyes and laugh for joy, as the absolute blindness and despair in which he had been buried alive for three whole days and nights was suddenly gone!

About two months later, Saul, and Ananias, the large brother who had been sent to heal Saul, were both walking through the night in Damascus for a different reason. The local Jews were out to kill Saul, since he had arrived to be their bloody enforcer, but had been converted to the most effective persuader for their opposition! The Jews in Damascus, like the ones in Jerusalem, were not big advocates for the concept of free speech, when the subject matter was the resurrected Son of God.

As they walked, Ananias and Saul compared notes, with quiet voices, of what it was like to have these miraculously healed eyes. Like Ananias, Saul had found that he also could see things beyond the veil of the material realm. There were things like seeing people as living, breathing, walking, talking fruit trees, some of which gave forth good fruit, and some of which gave forth poison fruit. There were things like seeing into a person's heart, and being able to directly see the emotions and hidden intensions buried deep inside, as though they were clearly written upon the person's face. At times, they could see the future that the good Lord had planned for the person, and could see them as they would become in time.

As the men entered the house of one of their brothers, which was located within the city wall itself, since he was a prominent local official, and was secretly a Christian, they moved smoothly and stealthily, not wanting to be observed, and thus cause their prominent brother a difficult time from their local enemies. There were three young men with them, brought along more for young muscle to do the lifting, than anything else. The boys had been sternly ordered to remain silent all through the mission, and they had obeyed. The two youngest of them knew enough to not argue with Ananias, since not too long before this night adventure, he had knocked them out for trying to rob him. The Lord had answered his prayer for them, and already they were serious enough about Jesus to be willing to risk a horrible death for His Name.

The men went through the house to the outer wall, and opened the one window in the wall side of the house that was mostly hidden from the top walk of the city wall. It would not do to have the city guards along the wall suddenly notice a man being lowered in a basket from the fourth floor window. The three young men and Ananias carefully lowered Saul down to the ground, where he climbed out of the basket, and carefully, but very swiftly, began to work his way out from the city wall, moving from bush to bush and rock to rock like some kind of silent, high-speed commando. Discovery meant death for all of them. Saul continued into the night toward the meeting place already arranged, where more brothers waited with swift horses to carry him far away before daylight.

Ananias smiled as he watched Saul from the window. Now when he looked at him he saw a strong, healthy young tree, green and whole, already yielding sparkling fruit of goodness that he left behind him with every step. Saul appeared as a brightly glowing, great, thick branch of a mighty Vine, and the fruit that fell off of him as he traveled also glowed in the night.

Ananias thought back to the day that his own eyes had been changed. It had been far to the south, in Israel, in his hometown of Bethsaida. Jesus had led him out of the town, and spit on his eyes, and ever since then, Ananias could see the normal world even better than ever, even though he was old, and he also saw through the veil of matter into the spirit zone. Jesus had told him not to return to Bethsaida, or tell anyone in the town that he had received his sight, but to leave forever, and start a new life somewhere else. Ananias had obeyed the Man Who had healed him, and since he had been pointed in the direction of Syria when told to keep going, he had continued walking for a while until he had arrived in Damascus. For the next decade or so he had been busy finding other believers in Damascus, as he started his new life there. He was one of the primary founding members of the church in Damascus, which was comprised entirely of converted Jews.

As Saul disappeared into the night, Ananias could hear the voice of Jesus in his mind saying, "Now you know why I sent you here ahead of time, to wait here to help Saul. I gave you back your sight, long ago, so you could be here now to help Me to give Saul back his sight as well. Freely you received, now you have freely given."

IF THINE EYE BE SINGLE

When the Lord was speaking about the single eye, it can be understood to be one of those multi-perspective wisdoms, for which He is so famous.

From the one perspective, He was likely advising us to maintain a single point of intense focus, if we wish to perceive the subject matter clearly, as in light versus darkness.

Those who are very familiar with the ways and means of human sight can tell you that we have instant auto-focus, and an eye-blink speed of less than a tenth of a second. They can tell you that we can discern a single candle in total darkness at a distance of fourteen miles. They can even tell you that wherever we look, our eyes lock onto the single point of interest simultaneously, in perfect sync, like a gunfighter with two six guns, firing both, at the same precise point, at the same precise micro second. If our eyes and brains did not perform like this, we would experience split vision all the time. So, in a very real perspective, as a physical function, our eyes must act as though they are a single eye for us to be able to see clearly.

Even though the brain itself, where all the visual processing is achieved, is comprised of two hemispheres, the brain must still function as a single processor, by means of the connections of the nerve bundle between the hemispheres, or we could not think clearly.

There is still another perspective to consider. He said "the light that is in you..." This would perhaps refer to the internal sight that we all have to some extent. Some have more than others, just as some people have better eyesight than others. It is nothing of which to boast, it is just that God has made each of us uniquely, and designed us with certain aspects, for certain reasons of His Own.

There is a sort of projection screen just behind the closed eyelids. For some people, it seems like a chalkboard; for some, it is like a large flat screen television. For others it is more like a large, open-air theatre, during a night time show under the stars. For some, it is like sitting on the very front row at the movies, right up by the screen; for some, it is like trying to see a confusing scenario, played out by indistinct figures, at a great distance.

Some folks see in color, some see grays, and some see black and white. Some perceive in two dimensions; some experience depth, also. For some, the viewing area is more like a long, deep translucent tunnel, in the starry night sky, showing things at vast distances in time and space. Sometimes, the observer is just observing; sometimes, participation is either required, or forced. Sometimes you see what you want, but sometimes you do not want to see what you do.

Sometimes things are symbolic, but sometimes they are literal. Sometimes they are specific; sometimes they are general. Sometimes things are clear; sometimes things are obscure.

When the human fetus is developing, the eyes form as buds that grow directly out from the brain. Over 98% of our total information input is visual. Most people think in pictures more than in words. For almost all of us, how we see is how we think, and how we think is how we see.

There is still another perspective to consider. The Lord told us that if our eye caused us to offend, we would be better off to pluck it out, and see righteously with the remaining good eye. Sometimes, we have to effectively remove our willingness to allow either eye to land upon that which our Lord does not wish us to see. If we cannot remove the beam from our eye, to see clearly, perhaps the eye itself must be changed, to perceive differently, and become filled with light again. One way the Lord achieves this is that, as He gives us new thoughts in new minds, we see with new eyes, and focus on new things. Remember, one of His most impressive miracles was when He opened the eyes of one born blind. In a very real sense, we are all born blind, until we are re-born of the Holy Spirit, and then we have spiritual eyesight, to clearly perceive the things of God. The natural man cannot understand the things of God.

The Word of God defines light as that which does make manifest, or visible. What is it that is made manifest, or visible, by light? It reveals anything that can be seen, either in the physical realm, or the hidden parts of creation. The Word of God defines Jesus as the true light which lights every man which comes into the world. This is not just speaking of physical light, but also of the light of understanding and wisdom. For us to be filled with light, we must try to remain focused upon the true light, Jesus. If we retain a single focus, upon the Lord, we will be filled with light.

PRISONERS OF FLATLAND

It all started quite some time ago. Some people think that the very first such occurrence was in some caves in France. That is possible, but it is far more likely that many others had already happened, only did not endure long enough to be discovered later, because they were done outside, where rain, wind, and abrasive dust (driven by wind) through the centuries destroyed all traces.

In more recent times, such things have been a part of human activity since people began building long-term shelter, and dwelling in permanent cities. There have always been paintings, drawings, carvings and all manner of artificial images made by the hands of men. Since men, and our hands, are made in God's image, we also have the ability to shape things with our hands, things which never existed before we imagined them, then made them. There was no space shuttle in the Garden of Eden, and no automobile, or bomb, either. There was also no painting, or drawing, or photograph, or videotape, or any such thing. God did not create them, since He knew they are not necessary for human life.

All of those images made by mankind are abstractions of something in reality, or distortions of something real. The picture does not actually free us to remember something, or someone, it ensnares us to have to lock our minds and our thoughts upon that one subject, person, event, or whatever is portrayed there, and robs us of freedom of thought in the reality of created things, and holds our thoughts captive in the abstract things made by mankind, instead of the real things made by God. That is the primary reason why the good Lord forbids idolatry, since mankind is worshipping something made, instead of the Someone Who made everything, and everyone, except Himself. God was never created: He always was, and is, and will be.

It is not only in Europe that such paintings have been found. They have been discovered and documented at Ayers Rock, in Australia, and in many places in the American southwest, and wherever else around the world that ancient people lived, if the climate remained dry enough, for long enough, or if the paintings were within shelter, such as the caves in France. There were also found similar caves with paintings in the Arabian Peninsula. The entire human race has always had a drive to make an image of something, because, being made in the image of God, we have many of the same drives and interests that He also has.

The Word of God states that no man can see God, and live. His glory is too great for mortal man to bear, ever since the fall in the Garden. If we humans, who cannot see God and live, try to make an image of what we think He looks like, how could we possibly be accurate? We have no model for our work. The Bible states that no man has seen God at any time. The only begotten Son of God has declared Him. You cannot be a man of God, unless you become a man of Jesus. God and His Word are ONE, and Jesus is the Word made into flesh. Jesus is God.

There was a mathematician in the 1800's who invented an imaginary place called flatland. All of the creatures that inhabited flatland were only two dimensional. They were things like a square, a triangle, a circle, and so forth. They could never escape the confines of flatland, even if it extended forever in length and width, because they had no third dimension to use for escape out. Now you can see a pattern.

When the enemy is allowed, by us, to lock our thoughts and minds into a computer screen, or a flat screen television, or a video game, or a picture, or a painting, or anything else that is not the real, live, three dimensional, surround-sound, high-definition, true-color experience of reality, as God has created all things, then we are accepting the counterfeit for the real. We should not allow the devil to cheat us out of the real experience of life, while we are still here to live it.

Perhaps the best thing for us, in our modern, 21st century computer-and-flat-screen world, is to use the technology as necessary, but not let it become a chain upon us. All things may be lawful, since Jesus paid our price with His blood, but not all things are helpful. We need to get out and see more of God's creation, not stay in with man's recreation. Instead of abstraction, or distraction, we need interaction with the Lord and the goodness of the things He made for us. At the least, we ought to thank Him more often, and think more about the things of God, and less about the things of man.

WORMWOOD

The young scientist rubbed his eyes, then his temples, then that stiff spot on one side of his neck. He put his glasses back in place, and checked his numbers for the fourth time, a process that once would require months, but now was finished in less than ten minutes.

People had realized that 2001 had forever changed the entire world, but this year, 2013, would change the world even more, and likely not all for the better. He had to decide, in the next hour or so, whether or not to scare the whole earth, or let some other scientist a few months or years in the future have the dishonor.

On the one hand, people should know, immediately, so they could make whatever sorts of last minute arrangements they felt necessary. Maybe the world's governments could do something to help at least some survive.

At that thought he suddenly laughed a quiet, dry, mirthless little chuckle. All of the world's governments working together could not possibly change the outcome of the next few years. Mankind does not have the capacity to just move planets and other massive space objects anywhere he wants.

This one was BIG, too. Anything which was heavy enough to actually bend light waves was not merely a gnat to be brushed away. It would have been spotted sooner, except that it was hidden somewhat by the asteroid belt. Three stars seen through the asteroid belt had been noticed out of position, all in a very close proximity to each other, as seen from earth. The computer running the telescope had noticed the error, and reported it. Upon further checking, it was not wrong, and the only thing which makes a star appear to jump around in the sky, even a little bit, is something as massive as a black hole, which can exert so much concentrated gravity that light waves passing near the massive object are actually bent by the warped space they are traveling through, or perhaps it could be some other point source of gravity, such as a neutron star. It would have to be tracked over the next few weeks, or maybe months, to try to detect its' precise vector, and calculate its' velocity, but, if it came anywhere near earth, or even the solar system in general, it could easily obliterate the entire solar system, including the Sun. It would have the effect of a second star, at least 2.4 times heavier than our Sun, or maybe much, much heavier, screaming through the system like the ultimate super freight train roaring right through our living room. If it did actually hit the earth, it would explode it, or gobble it up, like a small snack, without stopping, without even a burp, or perhaps bore a drill hole through it, without slowing down at all. If the point source turned out to be several smaller objects, like a gravitationally linked group of black holes, or neutron stars, then it could possibly even bore several holes in the earth at the same time, like wormwood.

"Wormwood…" That was a good name for it. He knew that the first scientist that makes a new discovery is allowed to name the new species, or object. He knew in his heart that he was about to tell his supervisor the disturbing news, in just a few minutes, when the older man arrived. He knew that hearing of it would make some people act very crazy, and some people act very sane, but he had a responsibility to break the news, anyway, or answer to God. Who had arranged for him to be the one who discovered the thing?

He then breathed out a great sigh, of both sadness, and relief. The possible outcome was sad, but at least he had made his decision. No matter how bad the news, sometimes it still has to be told.

THE UNITED STATES OF ISRAEL

The whole thing could be traced back to a promise that God had made to Abraham, and He later had also confirmed the same promise to Israel. Since Israel was the heir of Abraham, through Isaac, all of the promises and blessings of Abraham also came down to Israel.

The promise had been that whosoever was a blessing unto Israel, God would also be a blessing unto them. Back between 1917 and 1942, England was a great blessing unto Israel, after Theodor Herzl had persuaded Minister Balfour to draft and sign the Balfour resolution, beginning the process of the return of the Hebrews to Israel. During that time frame, England rocketed to world leadership and prominence even greater than it had ever known before. It was only after England slammed the gate shut (to stop Jews wanting to return to Israel, trying to escape the Germans) that the decline and fall of England began.

Even though Lyndon Johnson and Richard Nixon had other issues for which they were known, each one of those United States Presidents supported Israel in time of deadly war, and gave weapons to the Hebrews, to fight against their foes. There are many more Hebrews living in the United States, than there are Hebrews living in Israel, in these modern times. For the most part, all of the Hebrews in the United States are allowed to worship in their own chosen manner, without extreme persecution. Israel and the United States have become so interwoven over the years, that it would not be possible to separate them.

It has even become a normal bit of newsreel footage to see the enemies of Israel burning both the Israeli flag, and the United States flag, at the same time.

No other nation, in all the history of the world, has ever been so closely identified with Israel, without actually being a part of Israel itself.

When the United States helped Israel to survive in 1967, God rewarded the U.S. by allowing it to become the first and only nation in all of human history to actually send men all the way to the moon, and even safely return them. The reward arrived only about two years after the military help was given. Much big help was given, and so was much big reward. For better, or worse, God always pays back.

In the final years before the return of the Son of God to the Earth, all of the Arab nations, and Russia, and China, and even all of Europe, had very intensely wanted to invade and occupy Israel. They knew that they dared not even try such a thing, since the only nation in the whole world that could easily destroy all the other nations in the world would not tolerate that kind of foolishness. Without the U.S. standing guard for the survival of Israel, it would not take long for the rest of the world to pounce.

Some people have suggested that "the restrainer" (which holds the final war suppressed) is a reference to the Holy Spirit. This is possible, since the Holy Spirit is the Helper, not the hinderer. At any rate, the point is that "the restrainer" will be taken out of the way, and it is not possible for the Holy Spirit to be taken out of the way, since Jesus and the Holy Spirit are One, and Jesus promised that He was with us always, to the end of the age, and also guaranteed us that He would never leave us, or forsake us. Jesus is the Son of god, and the Son abides forever, and so He can never be taken out of the way, since He is the Way.

No, the Lord told us that by their fruits, we would know them. That means that the evil world is being restrained by the agent that is causing the restraining, and in modern times, that describes only the U.S. There is no other single nation that is single-handedly performing the safety functions of conflict suppression, negotiation, and resolution. Politically, and militarily, and until late 2008, monetarily, the U.S. keeps trying to keep the whole simmering world from boiling over, or exploding. The analogy which seems appropriate is like the carbon control rods in a nuclear reactor, to keep the runaway chain reaction from producing either a detonation, or a melt-down. An objective observer can also detect a similarity to a puppet show, with invisible yet powerful strings of manipulation for control.

The U.S. in the role of "restrainer" also restrains Israel from freely defending itself, and continually tries to make Israel give up its' own land to strangers, just to have a little peace in their own backyards. They even try to persuade Israel to divide up Jerusalem into sections, even urging giving away the Temple Mount, and all of the old city, just to placate a bunch of lying, murdering idiots. None of them ever should be called a suicide bomber, which is a lie. They should be called mass murderer, or maybe sub-human swine, or two-legged cockroach, or something like that. The most accurate description for that sort of nut-job is "devil-worshipper".

At any rate, once the flaming mountain did hit in the Pacific, the level of destruction done to the U.S. would be so extreme, there would be very little that any Americans could do, except pray, that might be of any help at all to Israel. As soon as the U.S. was effectively nullified as a dominant player in the final war, Russia, China, and the E.U. would rush in to fill the power vacuum created by the sudden crippling of the U.S. The gold rush would be on, headed straight for Israel.

There is an old expression of the world that states that when it comes to real estate, the only thing that matters is location. Israel had the location that was the crossroads of the world, and had unlimited potential for trade, mineral wealth, military advantage, and political leverage, and who knew what other yet-to-be-discovered riches might be found and plundered from the land of God's chosen people.

Every single power block in the world wanted to occupy Israel. Only the U.S. and Israel thought that the Hebrews should be the ones living there. Of course, once the U.S. had been taken out of the fight, Israel would be free to use all of their nuclear weapons, and a few special secret weapons that even the U.S. had never found out about. The only problem with that was this: after the U.S. was nullified, Israel would have to start using all of their weapons, within minutes.

The Arabs would rush in, because they were madmen that were warped into manic obsession with murdering all of Israel. The Russians would race them to do it first, since the Russians realized that that chunk of ground could force the Arabs to provide virtually free oil, and if that did not work, well, a few thousand Russian tanks, parked along the borders of Israel, facing outward, toward the Arabs, ought to be enough to persuade them.

The Chinese also understood the Russian war-logic, and were also ready to pounce. They did not want either the Russians or the Arabs to arrive first, since it would be much harder to install iron-fisted Chinese-style government if they had to first kill an enemy army, or two.

The E.U. wanted nothing to do with any of it, but could not afford to let the Arabs, the Russians, or the Chinese get that much of a strangle-hold on that much of the world's total oil supply. The E.U.

also had rapid deployment plans already in place for such a day. Europe did not suspect that the same series of cataclysms that would take out the U.S. would also take them out, within hours of each other. There would not be time enough for the E.U. to deploy anything, no matter how rapid they tried to be.

PAWNS WITH MINDS OF THEIR OWN

The whole thing had seemed simple enough in theory. After all, they had done it the same way, with smashing success, back in 1983, when the Iraqi dictator was about to finish his reactor. It would have been able to produce weapons grade output, and would have meant the end of Israel, less than two years later.

This time was much trickier, though, and had actually required the "look the other way" type of hidden co-operation the Egyptians had agreed to do, and then actually done. The Egyptians had a simple motive. If Iran became a nuclear power, there would be no more OPEC. Iran would just tell all the other Islamic nations what to do, and nuke them if they did not obey. Egypt could not allow that. Otherwise, the Dolphin-class sub from Israel could never have quietly squeezed through the Suez Canal, and around into the Persian Gulf. The one there now was not the same one that had first arrived, back in summer of 2009. Many different ones had exchanged posts there over the last five years, and all the time, a single authorized radio message from Tel Aviv could have pulled the trigger.

As technology had advanced, with geometric progression, surveillance equipment and techniques had also improved. The Israelis knew that with another month, Iran's reactor would finish making its' first weapons grade payload. They knew it would be plenty enough for at least a dozen bombs. They knew it would be no more than a few weeks after that when they could expect the first nuclear attack.

The order finally came. In the middle of the night, the sub launched a Tomahawk-class cruise missile, armed with a large, conventional warhead. It streaked at about fifty feet above the water toward the "secret" location of the reactor, until after a few seconds, it left the Persian Gulf and entered into Iran, a few miles north of Bandar Abbas. Most of the radar installations missed it, being set much higher, but some people on the ground noticed the screaming, flaming monster just a few feet above the ground, that appeared and vanished again in the blink of an eye.

Less than a half an hour later, a small solar flare seemed to appear in the night, right where the reactor had been, a few seconds before. The mushroom cloud it produced was not nuclear in proportion, but still impressive, nonetheless. The reactor was gone, along with a few hundred people that were working on it.

The same sub that had fired the missile had submerged again, and was headed out of the Persian Gulf, skimming the bottom in the shallow waters of the Gulf. At places, the water was less than one hundred feet deep. Just after the sub had slipped past Bandar Abbas, it intercepted more radio chatter, which was relayed instantly back to Israel. The translators there were stunned to hear that the Iranians had just ordered a full throttle, all-out suicide attack on everything in Israel, and the order was to leave nothing alive. Assad was commanded by his Iranian bosses to mobilize his entire Syrian army at once, and overrun Israel, not just infiltrate it the way they had done to Lebanon.

That put Israel with its' back to the wall, and no way out. Netanyahu and Barak, and all the rest of the modern-day Hebrew warriors, decided to end it, before Syria could. With little debate, and even less delay, the Israeli Army launched a ground based missile they had hoped to never have to use. Less than five minutes later, a very bright flash, far brighter than the sun would have been, except that it was still the middle of the night, lit up all of Damascus, and all the countryside around it for about thirty miles in all directions. All of the electronics and power in Damascus died immediately, as did every thing that lived in a flesh body, although the city itself suffered no worse damage than from a severe tropical storm.

Only two countries had ever perfected the neutron bomb technology that could perform such a feat. Israel wanted any intelligence it could find in Damascus, so, instead of vaporizing the city, they had sterilized the people out of it. Since all of the bacteria and viruses had also died, the dead bodies would still hang around a long time, slowly drying and turning to mummies.

Even though the weapon had done its' work effectively, it had been a very small one. The airburst over the city at five thousand feet had done the trick, but it still was detected by the Soviets, as well as the United States. The emergency phone lines across the world between the mighty leaders lit up in the next three minutes.

Putin slammed down the phone, and barked orders at his commanding general. For the first time in his decorated career, the general turned white as the blood drained from his face at what he heard. He stammered, "Yes, sir!" and turned to run do what he had been ordered. As soon as he had passed on those commands downstream, with much the same shocked response as his own, he went outside, and called his wife. He told her to immediately put the kids and the dog in the car, and head for their safe spot, hundreds of miles from Moscow. He did not know if he could ever get there to them, but at least he wanted them out the city right now.

The two men looked to the northeast, as a blood red sunrise stained the sky. Netanyahu asked Barak, "Do you think the Americans will come this time?"

Barak smiled a joyless, grim smile, and answered, "Maybe. Either way, the Russians will."

THE MOUTHS OF TWO WITNESSES

They had been at this war for almost three and a half years. They were not tired, in the normal sense of tired, since the present power of the Holy Spirit strengthened them. They were not hungry, since they had meat to eat of which others did not know, as the Master had also had, and their meat, as His had been a couple of thousand years before, was to do the will of Him Who sent them. They were never thirsty, since the Holy Spirit kept them continuously refreshed with living water. This was not just the situation in the spiritual realm, but the physical parallels were also being constantly given unto them. They did not sleep, but spent their whole time in prayer and thanksgiving, except when they were commanded to speak a decree to the whole world.

Their physical needs were met, and their defensive needs, also, since fire immediately consumed away any person or thing, even bullets in mid-air, if it tried to harm them. That had produced some really spectacular light and noise shows over the last three years, as the world had tried just about everything short of nuclear weapons to kill the two of them. Every time the prophets opened their mouths, and spoke their decrees from the Throne of Heaven, they first read out the list of charges against whatever person, or nation, or group of nations, or continent that had rebelled against God. Then, immediately, since the whole thing was being broadcast worldwide on many channels, in hi-def, and streamed online, the person or people knew that death was imminent, and there would be no escape, and no survivors. That is why almost everyone in the world was desperate to shut them up. The witnesses were present in physical bodies to witness for the Son of God, still in Heaven upon His Throne, in His Own physical body, at the Right Hand of the Father of Lights.

The fatigue they experienced was the endless foolishness of mankind, and the stiff-necked refusal to bow before God. The world just would not accept that no one ever stands taller, than when they kneel before God in prayer.

The hunger they felt was a driving need to see this whole war finished, and Jesus returned upon His earth, which He rightfully owns, lock, stock, and barrel.

The thirst they felt was a thirst for people to turn away from death, and return to God.

These men felt only one fear, though. They had a very minor concern that they might slightly misunderstand the orders God told them, and might not say precisely the correct prophecy. They had united together in prayer that this would never happen, and that they would complete their mission without error, or failure. The Lord spoke clearly to them both, at the same time, and they both heard Him promise them that He would not let them fail. They ceased (after He spoke) to experience any fear at all. After that, it was just serious concentration upon the task at hand.

There had been two active agencies, visible in the world, working to keep Israel alive and breathing for the last three and a half years. The most obvious one was the United States, which always, no matter who was president, stood by to defend Israel in actual military action, at least, if it were anything more than regional activity.

For over three years now, the two prophets had also fought a direct counter-assault against anything and anybody that made a hostile move in Israel's direction. Russia wanted it because they had a lot of Arab friends that wanted it, and if Russia owned Israel, it could pretty much have free oil from the Arabs. China wanted it because Russia wanted it, and two billion people used a vast amount of oil, anyway. Europe wanted it because it meant leverage and power in any trade or war negations in the future, both with the Arabs, and also the United States. Anyway one cut the cake, the choice real estate was still Israel.

The whole thing had almost gone melt-down nearly four years ago, when the Israeli intelligence agents had seen that Iran was about to achieve nuclear weapons. They had destroyed the reactor, as they had done in 1983 against Iraq. Syria had tried to launch a secret pre-emptive strike, to annihilate Israel, but Israeli intelligence again was quicker. This time, Israel used a neutron bomb, and could capture all the top secret data left behind in Damascus, as the Hebrew soldiers picked their way between the mummified corpses of the Syrians. Since even the bacteria had all been 100% sterilized, the bodies had not decayed, but had dried and shriveled, and were turning to dust. Russia had mobilized its' entire military, something the West had always feared, but also always prepared against. The Russians and the Chinese both came to a screeching halt in their mobilizations, when the United States, in a last gasp desperate measure to survive a nuclear war, destroyed every single Russian and Chinese submarine, and also every one of their so-called secret missile silos, all in less than three minutes. The whole coordinated blitz was a plan long in the works, for just such a day as that. The Russians aboard the Space Station had also been captured, and were being shipped down to military prisons, for espionage.

Ever since the prophets had been sent back from Heaven, in a chariot drawn by horses of fire, they had known just how long they had, and the day they would die. They could not wait. They wanted to finish, and return to Jesus.

Now the Holy Spirit revealed to them that the impact from the interstellar freight train known as Wormwood would occur very soon. The world had forgotten about Wormwood over the years since it had been discovered, since they had plenty of other things to deal with, thanks to the evil in the world, and the two good prophets. It also mattered that the star was dark, and horribly hard to see. If its' gravity had not bent the light rays from nearby stars, no one ever would have seen it coming. It had proven not to be the massive burnout that was at first thought, but had seemed much larger, because it was much closer. It had also picked up some freeloaders following after it, pulled along by its' strong gravity. These were mostly asteroids, and a couple of very large comets.

The prophets looked at each other, and smiled. These men had never met each other in this world, and had lived thousands of years apart in time. They were none-the-less true brothers, and Christians, and were grown close over the last years. A brother on the battlefield is a brother forever. They were glad they were leaving together, and soon.

Enoch had been the seventh generation descendant from Adam. Enoch had lived for three hundred years, early in the world, and Enoch walked all the days of his life with God, and Enoch was not, for God took him. Elijah had been a more famous prophet than Enoch, since there were vastly more people in the world in the time of Elijah. It was well-known, and witnessed by the prophet Elisha, and fifty sons of the prophets, that Elijah was carried still alive to Heaven, in a chariot drawn by horses of fire. No one had been standing there at the dawn of time to see that Enoch had been carried to Heaven in the precise same way. They were not "translated to a higher plane" as some unwisely have said, but they were both physically carried to Heaven, still alive, all without spacesuits. God proclaimed that nothing is impossible with Him, and He has been continually proving it ever since He first said "Be there LIGHT!"

There were unseen enemies wanting to attack and destroy the two prophets, also. They were not about to have any success at all, though, since General Tzedek-el of Heaven's Army, along with three hundred of his legionary commanders (which each commanded a thousand war-angels) formed an invisible, but impenetrable globe of protection around the two prophets, even extending under their feet beneath the ground. The two men were completely enclosed in safety, provided by a living shield wall of friends with swords, and laser cannons. Even heat and cold, or stormy winds could not break through to hurt the men, until their mission was finished. God just would not tolerate any interference about this matter. He was determined to give everyone on earth one last chance or two to repent, and follow Him. The evil hearted people in the world thought that He was being rough with them, but He was really trying to just wake them up to the fact that He was real, and alive, and would not allow evil to live, and Judgment was soon coming. The scope of the disasters had to be worldwide, so they would understand that the whole world would be judged.

Enoch closed his tired eyes for a few seconds, leaning his head back against the wall, and saw the impact from one of the flaming giant space rocks in a few more weeks. Elijah noticed and also closed his eyes. The two were shown a vision that was terrifying, and would have unhinged their minds, if not for the Holy Spirit holding them together through it all.

They saw a flaming mountain that had been an asteroid named Ceres, and it was about as wide as Texas. It hit near the equatorial region, between China and

Hawaii. The impact shook the whole planet to its' deepest core, and rang the earth like a bell. The resulting blast and tidal waves were of a magnitude that can only occur when things happen like planets smashing into each other at tremendous velocities. Over twenty percent of the Pacific Ocean, both North Pacific, and South Pacific, was immediately either splashed up into space, or vaporized into plasma and steam by the impact flash. Later, someone at a nearby star would have seen the earth flash brighter than the sun, as the heat generated would, for a short time, have been much hotter than the sun.

The men of Jesus opened their eyes, filled with tears, as they thought of all the billions that would die. They looked at each other, and their jaw muscles clenched, and they smiled a grim smile at each other, and Enoch looked up to Heaven, and said, "Father, please send our King back very soon!" Being in total agreement, Elijah said, "Amen!"

The two men heard the voice of God, as He said to them, "I have both sent Him, and will send Him again!"

CUMBRE VIEJA

It was one of those things that almost certainly had to happen sooner or later. The mathematical odds were just too great that it would eventually occur.

When the former asteroid named Ceres, about 625 miles in diameter, was pulled into the Earth's path by the passing dark star named Wormwood, perhaps everyone should have been relieved that the Earth would only be hit by a giant, high-speed, flaming mountain of rock as wide as the State of Texas. It could have been much worse. The dark star itself could have hit the Earth, swallowing it alive as it passed, without even a burp. The dark star could have hit the Sun, which would have produced something very spectacular, but not very likely survivable by the planet Earth, or us.

Instead, the good Lord, in His infinite mercy, directed the dark star away from Earth, though it still wrought havoc. It yanked about half of the asteroids out of their stable orbits, including the giant of them all, Ceres, and also captured Mars, as it screamed through the black night of space on the far side of the Sun, away from Earth. The Earth might have been kidnapped, or gobbled up, or sterilized, by the intense radiation (beaming invisibly out of the burnout star in all directions) as it passed.

As it was, Jupiter was also dragged along for the ride, and Saturn and Neptune were knocked out of their old orbits, and would eventually settle into new ones, much further out from the Sun.

Because of the intense, if very short term, tidal forces and gravitational interaction between the burnout and the Sun, the Sun erupted with extraordinary violence in the form of solar flares on the order of magnitude never seen in the

Solar System since the morning the Sun first lit up the night, and blew away most of the solid and all of the gas material from the four inmost planets. This time the flares were all directed right into the gravity well of the passing collapsed star, which promptly gobbled them up as though they were appetizers, and seemed to grow even hungrier, pulling in more and more streams of solar fire storms out into space, and making them vanish into blackness. The thing Wormwood had once been almost impossible to see, but now the stream of flares from the Sun made it possible to see the dark spot of the hole in space as it ate up the fire.

Ceres was pulled right into the orbit of Earth. Earth was built without brakes. When the two met, big, bad things happened, very rapidly. The impact was near the equator, between Hawaii and China. The resulting super tidal waves were miles tall, and had a period of many miles, also. About a fifth of the entire

Pacific Ocean became either steam, or plasma, or space ice. The shock wave traveled into and through the core of the earth, and the whole planet vibrated at subsonic frequency, like a giant, ultra, ultra-bass tuning fork. As the vibrations reached the opposite side of the world, only a few minutes after they started at the impact site, one particular island responded in a most destructive way.

At the north end of the Canary Islands, off the western coast of Spain, there is an island which is an extinct volcano. It is Cumbre Vieja, and the entire island, several miles long, is one giant, extinct volcano, which just looks like a big green mountain, with farms, and sheep, and goats, and things like that, and people, too, all over it. The sides are steep, but covered with much green vegetation.

Modern scientific imaging methods have shown that the island was already split lengthwise, from the north tip of the island, to the south. The split runs the whole way, and is hidden deep within the rock, covered by dirt, and green growing fields and trees.

The sudden increase in internal pressure within the earth, and the intense vibration, caused Cumbre Vieja to rumble twice, suddenly erupt violently, and split right down the middle, all the way through the cone of the volcano, down to the sea floor. The entire western half of the island, millions of tons of rock, slammed down to the sea floor, with the equivalent energy of several thousand atomic bombs. This was added to the already significant force of the eruption blast itself. The combined force generated a super tidal wave that raced westward across the Atlantic Ocean at three hundred miles per hour. The wave was going to arrive on the east coast of the United States in less than nine hours. It would announce its' presence as a two mile tall, forty mile deep, three hundred mile per hour power scrubber like the world had only one record of in the days of mankind. Something similar is recorded in the story of Noah. Another similarity is the red Sea closing with a slam to drown the Egyptians. It would drown and scour everything from the eastern coastlands of North America, and would also destroy much of coastal South America. The amount and force of the wave was going to cause it to travel hundreds of miles inland, submerging everything without the wings to fly away.

The people on the western coasts of North and South America would not be able to help those to the east. They would be dealing with problems of their own. The asteroid had generated enough ultra-tidal waves to destroy everything on the entire Pacific Rim, all the way up to the Arctic Ocean, where the force of the waves was still strong enough to break huge icebergs into many small fragments. Everything, and everyone, located anywhere on the western coasts of either

North or South America, was drowned, fried, boiled, choked with sulfur gases, or killed in some horrible way or other. No one escaped. No one survived, either. Only the interior heartland areas of the continents could survive, and not all of them did, for very long. All of Asia and the Orient also drowned for hundreds of miles inland. Since most of the population lived in the coastal cities and nearby regions, a significant chunk of the world's total population was washed away.

Mankind had been fouling the world with his filth for thousands of years, but the good Lord was still going to have the last Word. He had decided to use the oceans to scrub away some of the contamination.

The real, although admittedly very hard to perceive, purpose behind all the devastation was that God was trying to shock as many people as He could into giving up their resistance against Him, and to hear His Word, and do it. If some had to become an example, to show that He was deadly serious about the whole salvation and obedience commandments, then perhaps the rest would finally listen, and humble themselves, and pray, and turn from their wicked ways, and seek God's face, to get to know Him personally, and not just to seek His generous Hand for a hand-out all the time. God knew that time was running out. There was a countdown ticking that only the Father of Lights could hear, and He knew precisely when the right time would be to send Jesus back to judge the world. The extreme measures were the only way some of them would ever pay attention, and there was very little time left for them to respond.

YELLOWSTONE

There was a similarity between the magma dome and a tire with a weakened sidewall, where a large bulge, like a gigantic blister, stuck out from the rest, ready to blow. The last time it had exploded was over half a million years earlier. Over the last eighty years, one end of Lake Yellowstone had mysteriously risen up about thirty inches, in less than 100 years. Things do not change that rapidly in normal geologic processes, so something was definitely suspicious.

This thing was no ordinary, run-of-the-mill volcano. The underground sea of hot, melted rock covered most of the entire area of Yellowstone. It was a high pressure, ultra-high temperature, churning thick soup, and the pressure release had a cycle of about every 450,000 years, and this one was about

100,000 years overdue. The hidden monster was 40 miles in length, and 30 miles wide. It was the largest single volcano on the entire planet Earth.

It was not the only super-volcano on the earth, just the biggest. Lake Toba in Sumatra is another one, that exploded in the year 536 A.D., and changed the climate of the whole Earth, causing crops to fail, and people to starve, and kingdoms to fall, and new ones to rise, and made a permanent change to the climate of the mid east, and all of North Africa, changing what had for thousands of years been lush, fertile farmland into desert and wilderness, so the people either died off, or moved somewhere else.

There were many others, as well, including one in Africa, the entire island of Iceland, a place in Russia, the whole island complex of Hawaii, and several places in the Pacific ring of fire. All over the whole Earth, all of the volcanoes that in modern times were thought to be extinct, were only regarded so because no one had a record of them exploding recently. It certainly did not mean they could not.

When the dark star Wormwood had raced toward the Earth, it had remained hidden, both by being dark, and by being obscured for the most part by the asteroid belt. That was how it stayed hidden until it was only a few short years away.

When the giant asteroid, Ceres, had been dragged by the passing gravity of Wormwood into the path of Earth's orbit, it had managed a similar feat, hiding behind the moon until it suddenly jumped out from behind it into view, racing toward the planet. About six hours later, the asteroid Ceres would enthusiastically reunite with the planet of its' own birth, since Ceres had been the largest chunk of the Earth that had been blown away, at the moment the Sun had first turned on, with mighty force. In this case, the mother would not welcome the return home of the child. It was a mercy, in a way, that the asteroid approached on the night side of Earth, so fewer people were awake to see it and lose their minds from terror and panic. Those who did see it had quite a show, however. The thing was a gigantic ball of dazzling, flaming, solid rock, apparently trying to make a water landing upon earth, somewhere around the equator, in the Pacific Ocean, between Hawaii and China. It was about the size of the State of Texas, and if clouds did not obscure the view, everyone on the night side could see it, if they had been awake to know to look. The fire part of the show did not start until the monster entered the upper atmosphere, where it erupted immediately into a mind warping fireball that filled the whole sky, or at least, seemed to. The most spectacular part of the descent lasted only a few minutes, and then came the grand climax, at impact, with a flash that was hundreds of times brighter than the Sun at noonday. The air did not carry the sound of the impact, not as a sound wave, but as a super-compressed, rapidly-moving, steel-like wall of air, that knocked down and crushed everything in its' path at the rate of about a thousand miles per hour. This was accompanied by a blast of heat of over three thousand degrees, which immediately boiled all the surface layers of the sea as it raced over them. The sea itself was raised up into an outward expanding wall of water, several miles tall, moving at hundreds of miles per hour. The sea floor was left covered for a distance with nothing but bone dry, flash baked mud, and the rocky sea floor itself. Near the blast point, the air pressure dropped to near vacuum levels, as all the air and water were forced away, leaving only heat behind.

All of those changes could be seen from the surface, or near-earth orbit. The things which made even greater differences happened below the surface, and caused yet further changes to the surface and atmosphere. The Earth is about 8,000 miles in diameter, and Ceres is only about 625 miles in diameter, but, even though the Earth is 13 times greater in diameter than Ceres, it still caused quite a severe shock to suddenly have a long-lost chunk of Earth try to once more become "one with the planet", and as it drove deep into the center of the world, the internal pressure in the planet increased in a few minutes to critical levels, and continued to rise, as the kinetic energy from the impact was distributed throughout the planets' interior. Even before the asteroid came to a complete stop deep inside the Earth, rapidly melting from the magma's heat, the magma decided it had had enough intense squeezing, and found several ways to vent its' frustrations. Nearly every single volcano in the entire world (hundreds of them) instantly agreed to let out some pressure, to accommodate the magma. Had they not opened, the whole globe would have split down the middle.

The incomprehensible damage and death caused by the primary impact, plus the resulting tidal waves, and the Atlantic wave (caused by the eruption and collapse into the sea of Cumbre Vieja), meant that all the coastlines of North America and South America, and also the coastlines of anything in the Pacific Ocean were either already gone, or would be underwater, within a few hours at most. The shorelines would be drowned to death, inland for hundreds of miles. The devastation would reach from Antarctica to the Arctic. Australia would mostly cease to exist, as would Hawaii, Japan, thousands of islands, and even the east coast of Africa. Only the west coast of Africa would escape the work of the super-tidal waves around the world. Sea power would become a memory, since no shipping at all would survive the cataclysmic events. The things in the ocean which had flesh bodies could not survive long, either. Even all the plankton would be killed, and the resulting world-wide "red tide" would color the entire remaining oceans the color of fresh blood. Dead fish bodies of all sorts and sizes would cover the waters, and wash up on the uninhabited shorelines, where human bodies would be scattered in the mud, too.

Even with all of that, the human race still might have been able to possibly survive, re-organize, and re-build over time. Once the volcanoes joined the party, there was no chance left for anyone, though most did not consciously realize that fact, yet.

Yellowstone blew up, with a force almost a tenth as great as the asteroids' impact. Those two events produced such mighty earthquakes, that the whole earth rang like a giant bell. Almost every building taller than one story was collapsed, all over the world. Not one person could remain standing, no matter whom they were, no matter where they were. Even the dogs and cats were knocked over by the shaking, such as had never been seen since mankind was upon the Earth. The first earthquake hit when Ceres drove into the world, and just a few minutes later, when those that could try to stand up had made the shaky effort, the second quake hit, and knocked everything and everyone down again. The crust of the Earth danced like it was a living carpet, trying to crawl away.

The unimaginable blast from Yellowstone flattened, or melted, or both, anything and everything for almost a thousand miles all around it. Also racing outward from the eruption was a deadly poison cloud, of sulfur dioxide, and carbon dioxide, all carried out far and wide by the pyroclastic flow of 2,000-degree, super-hot, dense smoke. Many items, and people, were exploded, or burst into flames, if there was enough oxygen around them to support burning, but many items and people were flash-baked by the ultra-heat, without oxygen around them, and so were instantly dry-cooked, and preserved from decay, having been thoroughly dehydrated at once.

As the natural mushroom clouds from both explosions climbed higher into the stratosphere, the prevailing winds and jet streams pushed all the poisonous cloud southward, and eastward. The parts of the United States which had not been drowned by the oceans, or blown up or choked by the super-volcano, were not going to survive very long, anyway. It was not just the poison, and not just oxygen starvation, but a certain doom that would also claim the lives of everything that had a living body upon the Earth.

The entire island nation of Iceland also blew up, and produced similar results as had Yellowstone. From Iceland, tidal waves also raced outward in all directions, and slammed into all the coastlands of England, Denmark, Norway, and all the west coast of Europe, as far down as North Africa. The poison cloud from this blast also worked much death and destruction in that region of the world. The prevailing winds and jet stream pushed the cloud down toward all of Europe, bringing death with it.

The Mountain of Fire, in Goma, in the Congo, also erupted and killed millions, and sent out a great poison cloud, too, which headed east across Africa, killing along the way. It was being pushed, not only by the wind, but by the blast from the asteroid.

The water kicked up by both the asteroid impact, and the destruction of Iceland, meant that there would be a vast and dramatic increase in the amount of airborne water molecules. The extra dust launched into the atmosphere by all the volcanic eruptions meant that there would be a vast and dramatic increase in the amount of airborne condensation nuclei for the extra water molecules to find, and grab. There was going to be precipitation, on such an order of magnitude, as had not been experienced since the time of Noah. When it happened in the days of Noah, it all came down as liquid water. That would not be the case this time around.

One effect of the near-miss pass-through of Wormwood, disrupting the whole Solar System, was that the Sun increased its' activities to significantly higher levels, and poured out much more light and heat. For several weeks now, things on Earth had been getting very hot, and very dry. Crops were failing, water was hard to find, and nobody wanted to go outside in the extraordinary heat, since it was about 40 degrees hotter than normal, everywhere. It was springtime in Texas, but the last week had seen high temperatures in the 130 range. If this kept up, by July, 150 degrees might become a reality.

Most of the people in the world had been complaining against God, and even blaspheming horribly, as they blamed Him for all the trouble they had brought upon themselves. It never occurred to most of them to humble themselves before Him, ask forgiveness, and start hearing and obeying His commands.

God decided that He would cool them off, then, if they did not like the heat all that much. As the clouds overhead, heavy with liquid water, and dust, and ash debris, continued to thicken and thicken, the sky began to grow darker and darker. As this continued, around the clock, since the volcanoes were still spewing out ash and dust, the less and less sunlight was able to reach through the ever-thicker clouds. As less and less sunlight made it through, it not only grew darker, it began to grow colder. The average temperature dropped about 20 degrees for every twelve hours without sunlight. The change began slowly at first, since the Earth had been running hotter than usual, for over a month, and at first the darkness was just a heavy overcast, but it continued to darken more and more. By the end of the third day, the temperature had cooled down from about 130 degrees in Israel to about 50 degrees. By the fifth day, the temperature was about 20 degrees below zero, and all the lakes, rivers, and even large areas of the blood-colored oceans were beginning to freeze over, though it was too dark for anyone to see. From space, the Earth would have resembled Venus, both about the same size, and both completely white, covered by thick clouds. Venus had a hot surface, though, being closer to the Sun, and also having had time for the greenhouse effect to heat the planet up a lot.

As the temperature continued to drop, all of that extra water and dust in the atmosphere began to join up, as the lower air temperature caused the water to be forced to condense on something. Since the air is colder at higher altitudes, the stuff all just froze, and began to fall as every kind of frozen water, from the most tiny and delicate of snowflakes, all the way up to super-large hailstones out of the dark sky, some of which weighed more than a hundred pounds each. The additional destruction was almost the finisher.

The additional ice and snow upon the surface meant that any little trace of sunlight that tried to fight its' way to the surface would promptly be rejected by the white surface reflectance, and would produce no warmth at all.

By the end of a week, the temperature was about 100 degrees below zero, and still falling. If this cool down continued, within two more weeks, all living things upon the planet would be gone, and even the atmosphere would begin to freeze and fall into layers of frozen air upon the ground.

The entire population of the United States was already dead. They had all been buried in a nation-wide grave, covered in ashes and ice. Israel would remember them, but would have to count upon another Source of help from now on, in time of war.

THE LONGEST NIGHT

The Russian had survived all sorts of things. This situation was trickier than anything he had experienced, but it still had some potential for advantage, if he moved fast enough, and hit hard enough. There was no time to lose, so he called his commanding general, and issued severe orders. This time, the general hid his shock well, but he knew the leader was just as serious this time, as he had been when he had issued a very similar order, just three and a half years before. The only thing that had stopped those orders from being completed had been the Americans. They were no longer around. The general saluted, then turned and left.

Fifteen minutes later, the phone rang in the leader's office. The general confirmed that all the things were ready, and just waiting on the order from the top. The leader smiled, issued a very specific order, and then dialed the leader of China. He warned him to stand down, and not interfere, or face horrible consequences. The Chinese leader had his pride, too, and spluttered angry words and threats. The Russian listened for a few seconds, then interrupted, and said, "I have a deal for you." The Chinese stopped talking, and said, "Listening."

The Russian smiled into the video screen, and said, "We split it all, 50-50: the oil, the other mineral wealth, the food products, after the Sun shines through all this stuff, and whatever else we find when we get there."

The Chinese smiled slowly, and nodded, and said, "What's my part?"

The Russian answered, "Mobilize at once, your entire army, and head to the mid east. Do not go anywhere near central Iran, or down wind of it, since in another few minutes, it will no longer exist."

"Why are you killing them?"

"They vowed an oath to destroy all of Arabia's oil, and they're just crazy enough to do it."

"What about the oil and other things you are destroying in Iran?"

"Not destroying, sterilizing with neutron bombs. It will be useful again in six months. You must skirt along the border on the north side of Iran, where your army will be safe from our weapons, which we will only use in the south, and Tehran. Try to get to Israel in the next week, if possible."

The Chinese looked thoughtful a moment, then said, "Look, I know the Americans are gone, and all, and so is Australia, and England is almost vanished from the wave and blast from Iceland, but what about the rest of Europe?"

The Russian smiled, and said, "I have taken that into account, too."

The Chinese said, "If you are deploying nukes in Europe, are we going to be in the fallout zone? Just when are you planning to hit Iran? I need to know, precisely, so I can stay clear."

The Russian turned a bit, and looked at a small computer screen beside him. "You can proceed. Detonation will be air blasts, and will happen in the next fifteen minutes. See you in Israel. Oh, by the way, stay away from anything resembling large cities, or any sort of military thing, if they happen to be in league with Europe. They will be way too busy to interfere with us, and too weak by then to do anything, anyway. We will be too far south for the fallout to blow over us."

Within ten hours, after the Russian had confirmed the absolute sterilization of Iran, he called his Chinese accomplice again. After he hung up, he made another call, to his general. The man appeared in his office a couple of minutes later. He told him the next step he wanted done, and the general saluted, then left to comply.

The Russian called the Chinese back, and said, 'It's about to start. I thought you might want to watch the fireworks."

The Chinese said he already had cameras hooked up, so crank it up. The Russian made another call, and glowing columns of fire lit up the night all over Europe, producing a show of lights that the French would have envied, if it had not been killing them all. The entire continent lit up in the middle of the night, with a light that was much brighter than sunlight. The intense illumination shined up into the undersides of the thick black clouds, which made it look like the whole world was under a giant black roof.

Hundreds of millions of people were dying, but this disaster was not natural, but the work of demon-possessed madmen, an unnatural abomination that only did evil. Europe would not be a player any more in the military or

economic game for centuries, after this
night was done.

Even though the heat released into the
atmosphere by the hundreds of erupting
volcanoes might supposedly keep the
place from freezing to solid air, the loss
was faster than the off-set. Even several
dozen nukes, fired by the Russians, still
failed to heat the sub-zero world up
again. All the volcanic activity and
nuclear detonation was spreading more
poison than warmth, anyway. When the
Chinese started toward Israel, two days
after impact, the sky over head was very
dark gray, with wild lightning, and
strange storm patterns revealed in
snapshot format as the bright lightning
flashes displayed brief, surreal images in
the clouds, which never stopped
rumbling. The winds were wildly
unpredictable, and went from still as a
closet to hurricane force, with little
warning. The outside high temperature
was about 95.

As the monster army from the Great Wall, some 200 million troops, complete with mobile armor and artillery, raced its' way to the east, they saw signs of the destruction the Russians had achieved with only a few well-placed missiles. The Russian knew this would happen, and wanted his partner to get the point, that no one could oppose Russia, and not end up as dry corpses. The Chinese left the west border of Iran the fourth day after the impact, and the outside high air temperature was about 20 degrees. Men were not happy, and machines were also complaining. The machines they repaired. The men they dispatched, and left to freeze along the roadside. If more food were not found soon, the carnivorous army would begin to gnaw on its' own weaker members.

The Russians were also moving with mechanized speed to try to arrive first. They knew nothing would stop the Chinese from arriving there, ready for war and conquest. They could not allow the Chinese to settle in, by even a few hours, and secure the best strategic advantage, or they might decide that the Russians were no longer needed. The Russian had considered trying a secret head start, but knew that Chinese spy craft had come a very long way, and was sure it would not slip by unnoticed. It seemed better to include the Chinese, and later sort things out, once the oil had been captured. One problem was that nukes were off limits here, since no one wanted to damage oil production, except the mad Iranians, and they were all gone.

The Russians had started from a colder location, and were also dealing with the cold, but had vastly more experience with cold weather fighting, and using machines in extreme cold. As a people, they all had grown up far more familiar with, and adapted to, the cold, but it still was not a picnic. They did make better time, though, and would likely arrive a day or a day and a half sooner than the Chinese, which was just fine for the Russian. Within that day, he planned to capture all the oil for himself, and a small portion of his army was approaching Beijing, armed with strategic nukes, and another city several hundred miles further west than Beijing. The Russian planned to melt the second city, if the Chinese gave him any trouble. He would, of course, first notify them that even more tactical nukes were within range of the capital. (That ought to be enough leverage to make them cooperate, but a lot of things were different now, he thought, and by the way, just how cold is it going to get, anyway?)

Within five days, the Russians arrived, and easily conquered all of the Arab states, and all of their oil. The Hebrews would not go out easy, though, and fought as though they were on top of Masada once again, which, in a very real sense, they were. The Russians discovered that the Israelis had spent their time and their genius minds inventing and perfecting extremely effective weapons systems, and they used them very well. Every Russian missile that was launched exploded at ignition, killing all the crew of the launcher. At first the Russians just though it was a fluke, but when it repeated, every single attempted launch, for over 20 times, the hard-headed Russians gave up, and settled for trying to move the tanks and jeeps in closer. The Hebrews had answers for that also, and shined a special laser on the tanks, and the electronics and mechanics stopped working, circuits all fried. Sometimes, the tank ammo detonated, and the Russians stopped that after they lost 18 tanks, along with the crews. They decided to settle in and wait, until their buddies the Chinese arrived, the next day or so. No one had any airplanes left, and even if they did, who was going to try to fly them in a pitch-black blizzard?

Day six began, but no one could tell it was day. The temperature was about 110 degrees below zero. Even the Russians' machinery just did not work. People did not work, either, since more than ten minutes outside of shelter was inviting death. No one had ever felt a worse freeze, and no one had ever seen a darker night. All of the hope in every man's heart began to wither and die.

In the extremes of their distress, and locked in their madness, the Russians and the Chinese began to war against each other, each side claiming the other side had betrayed them, and led them all here to die. Those statements were almost correct, but it was the devil that betrayed them all, and led them all there to die. They all did die, too, as they fought hand-to-hand against each other, where they had camped next to each other only a day earlier. The entire Valley of Megiddo, the strangest battlefield in the world, began to actually fill up with the blood of all the dying, as more and more of them pressed into the valley, trying to win the fight for their side. The bizarre scene was illuminated by the constant gunfire and explosions of grenades and artillery rounds. The roar of the conflict was deafening. Hebrew Christians watched from the top of Har-Megiddo, the mountain that overlooked the battlefield. They knelt and prayed that if any of the people down on the battlefield could be saved, even if it had to be seen later, when they were resurrected, that the good Lord would see their hearts, and not let them go to the fire.

Immediately, the Hebrews clearly heard a Voice out of thin air, not exceedingly loud, but extra clear, and somehow sounding like the roaring of a great waterfall a distance away. The Voice said, "Nevertheless, when the Son of man returns, will He really find faith on the Earth?"

As soon as the voice had finished speaking, a sudden great light flooded the whole world, making everyone stumble and fall down, holding their hands over their eyes form the dazzle of it. The light was not like a sunrise. It came from directly overhead, if anything, a little from the east, and it was moving rapidly to center over them. It came to a stop right over the praying Hebrews. The sound of a mighty trumpet was heard, a shofar the size of Florida, being blown by a cherub the size of a small planet. The frozen earth shook violently, and cracked open yet more volcanoes, and the almost frozen air seemed to somehow crack apart, also. The frozen seas and all the whole Earth released all of the saints, believers in Jesus, both the still alive in their bodies, and those being instantly resurrected. All of the saints were changed into glory, and raced to meet the

King of Kings in the sir, and join up in the army of Heaven. The darkness of the sky began to splinter into pieces, which withered into thread-like wisps of darkness that seemed to be blown away by the King of Kings and His overwhelming Eyes of Living Flame. The entire Army of Heaven and all the saints that had died in the Lord were returning to clean the earth forever! The angels of God flew out everywhere, faster than eyes could perceive, rounding up anyone they saw that had an evil heart! The Saints of God, all dressed in pure white war-armor, and riding horses of fire, came thundering down onto the battlefield, chasing down and killing the enemy soldiers they saw with wicked hearts! In this horde of killers, there were none that the Lord counted guilty that would be spared. The soldiers of the Army of Heaven could see a blue-white light around the head of each person that was to be spared, and they made no mistakes at all. The soldiers did not arrive alone, but were also helped by millions of war-angels, and even the three mighty, good cherubs came to fight and bind the enemy dragon. The evil people cried out for death, but death had already been rounded up and bound, also, along with hell. The mighty cherubs did not need long to overcome even the most stubborn of enemies.

At the head of the charging column of avengers rode the Son of God in His full glory, and His radiance blinded the sight. The voices of the whole Army of Heaven were chanting again and again "HOLY, HOLY, HOLY!"

The wicked could not outrun the angels. Soon the evil were gathered together in bunches, held bound by unbreakable golden chains of justice. Any one of them would have gladly killed for this much pure gold in any form in their evil lives, but now they did not like it so much, as they could not escape it, and they could never spend it.

Then a very mighty angel, actually the great cherub of time, Gabriel, came down from heaven and stood with one foot on the land, and another foot resting solidly on the sea, and he shouted with a great, world shaking voice, "There shall be time no more!"

As soon as he had said this, every single timepiece known to mankind broke, and fell to pieces in dust. Exceptions were the atomic clocks, which just went inert and cold, dead, instantly. Time had always been the temporary condition, a thing made for a purpose by God, until its' purpose was done. Now the purpose for time had been fulfilled, and God had finished His strange work, and eternity continued on just as it had always done, before time, and now, after time, also. There would be no more winter, no more night, and no more darkness, for the Lamb of God is forever our Light.

A great voice was heard again from Heaven, the voice of the cherub of eternity, Gabriel, and he shouted, "Now are the kingdoms of this world become the kingdoms of our Lord, and of His Christ!"

HE SAID BE LIGHT, AND HE MEANT IT

The invincible Army of Heaven was streaking like living missiles of fire toward the Earth. The resurrected saints came riding horses of living fire, without being burned, or, in some special cases, they were mounted upon resurrected horses and donkeys which had been promoted to the greatest war-chargers of all eternity.

The Son of God was at the very point of the Spear of Justice, returning, as fast as light, to kill the wicked forever, and wrap up this "refinery-of-human-faith" project, which had been one of the primary reasons for the entire Creation. It was faith that the Father had had to refine by the fire of tribulation, and persecution, through pain, and suffering. Once people had fought their way through the fire, made possible only with the Help of the

Holy Spirit, their motives and priorities were purified before the Lord, in righteousness. Then the Lord had what He wanted from us all along, which was steadfast, faithful patience, and obedience. All He commands is for people to let God be God, as He really is, and obey His Word. If we goof up once in a while, He forgives us, and tells us just to quit doing it, make restitution, and move on to the next phase.

The earth looked like a giant white tennis ball to the eyes of the approaching Army. The impenetrably thick clouds of gas from the impact of Ceres, and the resulting worldwide upheavals, and volcanic eruptions, worse than any since mankind had walked the world, had blanketed the Earth in a solid white burial shroud, making the planet a fairly close twin of Venus. The major difference was that Venus had a surface temperature of hundreds of degrees, and Earth had a surface temperature lower than a hundred degrees below zero. Beside that, Venus was not inhabited by living flesh, but Earth was. If the King of Kings, and His entire Army, were not returning right now, no living thing on the planet (that dwelt inside living flesh) would be able to remain alive much longer. The final sterilization of Earth was less than a day away, otherwise.

The people under the clouds could not see anything but darkness, unless it was a flash from some manmade weapon or other. There were a lot of those flashes, and they lit up a dark, thick overhead roof of black, solid clouds, filled with thunders, and many lightning streaks. They were all freezing to death, or choking in the toxic fumes in the atmosphere, or killing each other at the slaughterhouse of the world, which is the battle plain at Megiddo. Over a third of a billion people were there, all trying to be the last man standing, or wading, through the huge lake of human blood, which had become chest-deep, in places. The blood was freezing over, even as more was continually spilled upon it, and only the fact that the fresh spills started out at 98.6 degrees had kept the lake of blood melted so far, as this had been going on all night long, the seventh night since Ceres slammed into the Earth. When an asteroid 625 miles in diameter lands, it makes a few big changes around it. Living flesh is fragile, and does not accommodate extreme changes very well.

The few Christians left alive upon the world were locked in battle, struggling, in prayer, to help to turn the tide, and to actually persuade the Lord Jesus to return to save the remaining human lives left still alive. Most had already died. Those Christians could not know it for certain, but each one of their hearts felt His rapid approach, and they suddenly prayed with renewed intensity, and hope, and with a growing, joyous smile in their hearts, as millions of people were dying all around them. The Christians that died in battle were immediately included into the Army of Heaven, stunned to instantly wake up on a horse of living flame, in an unbreakable body, racing toward the battle ahead. In a fraction of a second, they each knew and understood what this was all about, and joined fully in the spirit of the attack.

Off to the right of the Army, the Sun was acting strangely, burning at a much greater intensity than normal, and was snaking out huge solar flares like tentacles into the passing dark star, named Wormwood. The Lord Jesus looked directly at the Sun, and said, "Settle down!"

The Sun immediately obeyed, and returned to normal operations, in the blink of an eye. The Lord Jesus looked directly at Wormwood, and said," Your purpose is finished. Be gone!"

The dark star immediately vanished, into thin space, not thin air. It left silently, and Mars, Jupiter, and the other captives the dark star had captured were suddenly released from its' no-longer-in-existence gravity field, and they all began to find their ways back into orbits around the Sun.

The Army was nearing the Earth. They were only about as far away as the moon, and their rate of travel began slowing as they neared the world. The Lord Jesus focused His white-laser Eyes upon the planet, and said," LIGHT!"
The precise point where His stare was locked, the peak of the Mount of Olives, began to glow with dazzling bright light, as the clouds over Jerusalem began to burn through from the unstoppable white laser beams of His mighty Eyes. The clouds melted away as the Army arrived, and the world began to be illuminated, from directly over Jerusalem, with a brighter light than had ever been seen there before. The Lord Jesus shouted, "Gabriel, blow the seventh trump!" The

mighty cherub Gabriel blasted a deafening, earth-shaking, seemingly endless note from a gigantic shofar, and the shaking Earth opened all the graves of the saints, and the frozen sea split in millions of places, to let out the dead believers in the sea. All of God's people from all of time, all over the world were raised at once, and changed to great glory, having the appearance of little brothers and sisters of the King Himself. All of the saints, whether just resurrected, or still alive in their original bodies, rose upon mighty new wings to meet with the Lord and all of the Army of Heaven as it neared the Earth. All of the people upon the surface had either a reaction of extreme joy and thanksgiving, or extreme terror and vain attempts to outrun the hundreds of millions of good angels that were also there openly, as part of the Army. The Lord Jesus had ordered the good angels to go round up every wicked thing, and bind it unto Judgment. The good angels flew out all over the earth, and all over the sky, too, arresting every evil-hearted creature, and bunching them together to be burned.

Surprisingly enough, there were still many Christians alive upon the Earth. There had never been any such event as a pre-tribulation rapture-type escape from the world. Since the Resurrection of the Lord Jesus, no Christian ever left the world, except by death, until this Day of Days. Before the Lord had come (indeed) in the flesh, Enoch and Elijah had each been carried to Heaven, each in a chariot drawn by horses of living fire, but that had been for a special purpose, which they both had just finished fulfilling as a team, and now, after their own deaths, those two mighty war-prophets were riding back to the Earth along with all of the rest of them.

Now the dead saints had risen whole and well out of their graves, and were changed into magnificent, beautiful creatures, just like the Lord Jesus in appearance, if not in full glory. The remaining Christians in the world were also changed into resurrected glory, and also began to fly on spectacular new wings upward to meet the King of Kings in the air. Everything was happening at once, with dizzying speed, as all of the ancient prophecies from Holy Scripture were being completed and fulfilled at once.

As the resurrected-unto-life people were flying upward, the evil people were being rapidly rounded up and bound by the arresting angels, before they could escape or hide. All remaining people from everywhere in the world, including all the oceans, or the ice, which had once been oceans, were being gathered together. All of the people were thinking they had made it okay, until the majority of them, being the evil-hearted ones, were grabbed and carried off by the good angels, which were very busy, even though they moved at ultra high-speed. The whole earth, though covered in ice and snow, had been extremely ugly when they first arrived, since all of the ice and snow had volcanic ash and dust mixed into it, in such concentrations that it not only made the particles bigger and more deadly when they had fallen, it had also darkened them to various shades of gray, so that the whole effect was very dreary. Once the King of Kings had entered the atmosphere, the whole thing changed to clean white again, with the oceans beginning to melt very rapidly, and turning back to healthy blue. The grim death-clouds overhead were thinning, and all turning cheerful white. As the clouds continued to thin, the sun could finally be seen again, low on the eastern horizon, and blood red. It was the morning of the eighth day, the same as Resurrection Morning, almost 2,000 years earlier.

As more and more light flooded back into the world a profound change became evident. The veil between the seen and the unseen had been removed, and everyone could clearly see all of the whole creation, and every creature included in it, too. People could see the Lord, in His true glory, and they could also see the good angels, and the good cherubs, too. They could also see the devil and his evil angels. They were able to watch as the good angels chased down and bound all of the bad angels, and then there arrived the mightiest good cherub, Eden-el, who had not been mentioned in Scripture ever since he had been stationed as the mighty guard at the Gate into the Garden of Eden (since he was the strongest creature ever made, and everyone else combined could never overcome him). He was the Cherub of Energy, with which the Lord had made all the other aspects of Creation, being time, space, and matter. They watched as he grabbed the former cherub of matter, now the worm, and bound him with an unbreakable chain of Justice.

As the rest of the wickedness was being thoroughly purged, piece by piece, from out of the Earth, the entire world was being restored and transformed into what it once was, and should have always remained. The air was rapidly becoming clearer, and cleaner, and the hope of the good creatures was finally becoming a reality. The Earth was beginning to be totally rebuilt, and healed, as the Lord was fulfilling His prophecy that He would make all things new!

MANY FIRST SHALL BE LAST

This latest atrocity was not the first horrible thing done by the insane pervert Herod, but it would most certainly always be remembered as the worst. The puppet for the Romans was so vain, twisted, and insecure, (knowing deep in his evil heart that it was all just a lie, and knowing he had no valid right to be called king, and his own people hated him with a cold, deadly disgust), that he would hold himself back from nothing to keep his grip on power.

His people already loathed the very sight of him, and his sudden murder of twenty four little boys, (all two years old and younger, even including a new-born), would have been plenty enough all by itself. They all had done not one single thing wrong in their short lives, except to have the misfortune to be the youngest boys in a small town of a few hundred people. The crazy jerk of a tyrant had had them all killed, trying vainly to overcome the Holy Word of God, as delivered by the mouths of all His Holy Prophets.

The King of Israel did indeed appear first in Bethlehem, just as foretold. By the grace of God, the Son of God escaped the attempted assassination of Himself, the new-born King of Kings. The other twenty four little boys of Bethlehem had a different future in store, but the Almighty God of Heaven did not for one second forget them, not even a single one.

About three thousand years later into the future, the King of Kings had been reigning openly upon the rebuilt Earth for a thousand years. Evil was banished forever, and could never possibly return at all. Things were right again, and clean, and whole, and pure, and delicious! It was all like the Garden once more, and this time the Garden covered the whole earth, and men and animals lived in peace with each other, and all lived in peace with God. In the enormous city of New Jerusalem, which covered about as much ground as Alaska, the awards ceremony had been going on for a very long time. For the better part of a week, millions of people and all other sorts of good creatures had been walking single file before the Throne of the King, and He blessed each one of them by name, with a special reward that most perfectly pleased both the King, and the person to whom He gave the reward. These rewards were not temporary, but eternal, and even though He was astoundingly generous with everyone, He never ran out of more wonderful things to do and give to each good creature. They were, each of them, stunned, and overflowing with thanks, as they moved on by to let the next people in line have their moment with Him. As the very, very long line finally began to shorten to just a few hundred people left, a noticeable change had begun. These last folks coming by were some of the mightiest warriors of faith that had ever lived. Among this group were notables like Noah, Job, and Daniel. Also there were Hananiah, Mishael, and Azaria. Moses was also in this group, as was Abraham, and Abel, and Jacob, and Joseph. Ezekiel, Isaiah, David, Solomon, Joshua, Caleb, Gideon, and Esther were also in this last group. The apostles were there, and so were the rest of the sons of Israel. Paul was among them, too, and seemed a little bit star-struck as he stared in amazement at all the super-heroes of faith that stood with him in line. Enoch was there, and Elijah, and John, and John the cousin of Jesus, too.

There also was the one known forever as the "thief-on-the-cross", as well as King Hezekiah.

Each one of these last people received rewards the human mind could not quite completely understand, but they all knew that whatever He wanted to give to them would be something they would cherish forever. They each one knew they would always have their main dream, anyway, which had always been to love the Lord, and to stay with Him forever. At the very final end of the whole line, twenty four men approached the King as one close group, and stopped before Him, and bowed their knees to Him, and each one cast down the magnificent golden crown that the King had already given to each of them, a thousand years earlier, when He had resurrected all the martyrs. They tossed those spectacular crowns before His feet, and bowed to their faces before Him, and shouted "Holy, Holy, Holy!" as they worshipped Him, and all the creatures in Heaven, and upon Earth, now joined into one Kingdom forever, with one King forever, began to also praise and glorify Him. After a few minutes of the sudden uproar, He gently, smiling, motioned for them to hold on for just a second.

Then He spoke directly to the twenty four men still bowed down before Him, and said, "Stand up, My friends! You were the first martyrs for My Name's sake, once I had come into the world. As you were the first for Me, so now I honor you last, and most. Take your places of authority, and rule with Me, over Heaven and Earth, and be forever known and honored as the Twenty Four Elders!"

FULL SPECTRUM

Poverty, or treasure,

Misery, or pleasure,

Joy, or sorrow,

Today, or tomorrow,

Heartbeat, or breath,

Even Life, or death.

We thank You, Father, Maker
of Heaven and Earth:

You're giving us all these blessings, from even before our birth.

FOR RICHER OR POORER

People do not want to hear bad news. At least, they do not want it to be about them personally. When the group of terrorists from the mid east first attacked the World Trade Center in the 1990's, with a bomb in the basement parking garage, no one wanted to take it seriously, being blinded by pride. After all, wasn't this the country that had sent men to the moon, and brought them back alive?

People thought no more about the terrorists, until a little after nine in the morning on 9\11\01. By noontime that day, no one was laughing about stuff like that any more. No more airplanes were flying in the sky over the United States, except U.S. fighter jets, hunting for targets. The world changed suddenly, in the blink of an eye. It was not until we saw the second plane ram into a building that our minds went numb with shock for a few seconds, while each of us tried to figure out what had just happened. Some of us were already praying for the folks in the first tower, and this made it even more urgent. Maybe even more would have died, if we had not been praying for them. At any rate, everyone now understands just how deadly serious a threat the extremists have proven to be.

Another noticeable effect of the Twin Towers murders is that almost every house in the U.S. suddenly sprouted an American flag, and all the church pews filled to capacity. Hmm. Do you wonder if God also noticed the same thing?

Maybe we should not wait until the next catastrophe to start praying, and studying our Bibles again. Maybe we should start every single day with at least a few minutes of sincere prayer. Maybe we should pray quietly and discreetly all through the day, as the Holy Spirit leads us. Maybe we should have, as our first meal each day, a cracker and a cup, blessed in the Name of the Lord. Maybe we ought to act right now as though our very lives depend upon our close relationship with Jesus, through the Scriptures, and the Holy Spirit, and our humble obedience.

Since it is for certain that God made Heaven, and Earth, and all that is in them, and all of us that live and breathe know that our breath is in His Hand, it is clear that no one can get along without God. The challenge is for us to get along with God, since He is always right, and, if we disagree with His opinion, about anything, then we are always wrong. The Word of God states that there is no wisdom, or understanding, or counsel against God. God is never wrong, even a little bit. Anyone that disagrees with Him is, by definition of terms, wrong. Ever since the events in the Garden of Eden, it has been difficult for men to agree with God. We keep thinking we know better.

When the children of Israel were still in Egypt, they were worked very strenuously by their Egyptian over-seers. This intensified near their escape, as they had to make the bricks without being given straw, which meant they had to gather their own straw, as well as keep up with the brick quota. This ran them ragged, but toughened them to resilience. The Word states that when they were led out by Moses, there was not a feeble one among them. They had all had plenty of Egyptian food, since their captors had known that the slaves could not work, unless they had enough strength to do the work in the hot sun. The extraordinary exercise, over a period of time, made them each mighty, if they did not die from it.

They were strong enough to make it through the wilderness, and survive in it until they all had passed away, but left behind their children, who had grown up desert strong, and who were ready to follow God, along with Joshua and Caleb, into the Promised Land, even though it meant much war along the way. They were also ready to win the war, and they did, but only with the direct help of Almighty God.

Around the whole world in 1929, a terrible thing happened. Money and jobs suddenly became scarce, and stayed that way for the next twelve long years. Different people, both as individuals, and entire nations, responded to the financial catastrophe the way they thought best, but all of their so-called wisdom proved not so wise. Some nations spent whatever resources they had left in a mad arms race, with every developed nation trying to produce unstoppable weapons. Some nations wanted them for defense. Some figured the way out of financial trouble was to invade their neighbors, and steal everything they owned. Those heartless bastards did not care if the neighbors had to be murdered to accomplish the invasion. Some entire nations, and almost all of their people, became murdering thieves. Now, after twelve tough years of depression, the good people in the world had to fight and kill two-legged monsters that were pretending to be human. The good folks were tough enough to fight the war, and win it, and they did, too, but only with the direct help of Almighty God.

Now, everyone is all upset about the current economic conditions around the world. No one stops to consider that Almighty God, Who is aware of and in charge of everything that exists, knows that we are having trouble buying gasoline, and paying our mortgages, and trying not to lose our homes. He knows that we are struggling, and He would not allow the devil to bother us this much, if He was not eventually, sometime ahead, determined to bring good out of the evil the enemy tried to do. That is the hallmark, and thumbprint of our Lord upon His work, that however it starts out, no matter how horrible, God is still able, and willing, to bring good forth at the end of it all. The worst thing that ever happened was the murder of the Son of God. God has brought the greatest blessing possible forth from that terrible event, and caused the salvation of all the saints, which could not otherwise have happened.

Did anyone stop to wonder what it would be like, if you had plenty of money, but could not buy anything with it, unless you let the store scan your microchip under the skin on the backside of your hand? Would it mean more to you to have the groceries, or your freedom? What if the gas pumps would not operate, even with cash, unless you first let them scan your chip?

It might not be an actual physical chip, but an electronic tag, keyed to your face, and name. Computer technology has been applied to face-recognition programs, which have grown stunningly accurate, and lightning-fast. This has changed the science of tracking an individual and their movements. The technology already exists, and is in use in trouble spots around the world, tracking enemy ring leaders, and allowing them to be taken out with surgical precision. Even if they get two of the guy's buddies along with him, they are absolutely certain they do get the right man. Beards, head garments, and the like do not have much of a chance to conceal the target from these ultra-advanced computer programs. Increased high resolution video cameras are also an essential component in these things.

So, if it seems that times are getting tougher, well, they are. We have been honestly promised that it will become so extreme, that it will be a grisly struggle, just to stay alive in flesh bodies. Perhaps we must learn to give our Lord thanks for His goodness to us, in that He uses the tough times we are dealing with right now to strengthen us for greater wars, further on down the road of time.

In the book of James, we are instructed to count it all joy, when we face trials and tribulations, since it will produce in us patience, and perseverance. I know those are the things God wants me to have in my heart, and manifest outwardly to others, as encouragement also to them. A lot of the time, I still feel like the little kid in the back, in my little car seat, vainly turning my little plastic steering wheel this way, and that, but the car just keeps right on going down the road. So, in frustration, I try to honk my little toy horn on the little toy steering wheel, but it is only a fake horn, and does not honk. So, finally, in absolute frustration, I begin to ask, over and over, "Are we there yet? Are we there yet?"

Ever notice how the Driver does not answer? Not a Word is uttered, until, at long last, when all hope is nearly dead, the Driver stops the car, and opens the door, and lifts me out in big strong arms, and says, with a happy smile, and loving Eyes, "Yes, we're there yet!"

ABOUT THE AUTHOR

People have sometimes asked me why the Lord is such a big deal to me. Jesus told us Himself, when He said that whoever is forgiven little, loves little, but whoever is forgiven much, loves much. The good Lord has forgiven me very much. I was never a violent person, or a person trying to work wicked schemes against others, but when I was younger, during, and sometimes after, my Navy years, I was certainly not what one could consider a "goody-two-shoes".

One of the changes I have noticed in myself over the years is that different things matter to me now, and things that once seemed worth effort and attention, and money and time, have been replaced (in my internal priority list) with things that actually do matter much more.

The Lord has allowed me to understand a fascinating viewpoint. Even though I intend to spend all of eternity with Him, when either my time in this present world is done, or when He returns, if He wills it that I survive in this world that long, I still will only have one precious chance in all of eternity to glorify Him, when no one can now even directly see the One I seek to honor. To give it to Him now, cheerfully, is obedience, performed in faith, given in love for Him. Commandment number one says that we are to love Him.

Do not think that I believe myself to be good. If I could be good, Jesus would not have had to die to save me. I just want to honor the One Who is so good to all of us.

EXPLORING THE UNKNOWN WOODS

Most of the time, we love to travel the same old familiar roadways. We go to and from work, play, shopping, maybe even church. We like knowing that we are going to end up where we expect, without any surprises.

Studying the Word of God can be a bit like that, too. We like familiar old lessons, and sermons, and the same old well-known passages again and again. Such things can be very comforting. I miss the old hymns we used to sing when I was growing up.

Sometimes, we see a glimpse of something mysterious off to one side, hidden by trees. Usually we do not take time to explore. My attention has been drawn, over and over, to some of these mysteries. I prayed that the Lord would go with me to explore, and help me understand, and keep me still on course with Him. I remain sincere, to write what He shows me. He made sure that the story ideas (mostly from dreams) would not stop until I wrote them down. This is what I saw.